We were forced to live with Mama Lelethu Nala in our house from 21 August 2020. It was after the court determined that, although she was the new owner of the house, she could not just throw us out on the street – it would be dehumanising. Eviction proceedings could not go ahead while the country was in a national state of disaster because of the Covid-19 pandemic. But, as the owner, she also had the right to take possession of her property. We were all shocked by the strange ruling that Mama Lelethu could move into her house even though we were still living there. And that is when all the trouble started.

Two years prior, our house had been sold to Mama Lelethu against our will by the bank. My father had been retrenched from his job at Eskom, and was unable to pay his bond. The bank then decided it would recoup its money by auctioning off our house. My parents had been living in the house for eighteen years, since before I was even born. I had lived there my whole life. Now it was no longer our house, according to the bank.

Mama Lelethu had tried on several occasions to evict us. She had sent letters from her lawyers and exhausted many legal and illegal means to force us out. Knowing that a court order for our eviction would take time and money to obtain, and would entail many stipulations as to how the eviction was allowed to take place,

7

she had opted to send some thugs at night to remove part of the roof while we were sleeping. The thugs only managed to remove a few slates. They were caught and beaten up badly by my father and members of the Protea Glen Extension 11 community. No one was arrested. My father had some connections at the Protea Police Station. From that day he had threatened to kill anyone who tried to occupy what he still called his house.

After that incident we lived peacefully for about seven months before Mama Lelethu hired a bulldozer driver to break down our wall. My father went to court protesting this illegal action and he actually won that case. The court said our squatters' rights to property, family life, dignity and equality had been violated by Mama Lelethu's act of vigilantism. She was ordered by the court to rebuild our wall, which she obeyed grudgingly.

After that, Mama Lelethu changed tack. She said that if we wanted to stay in the house we could do so, but we had to start paying rent. My father refused.

One morning, at the beginning of 2020, Mama Lelethu came to the house with an entourage of two bodybuilders. My father didn't even allow them beyond the gate. Instead, he stood on the veranda and pointed a gun at them. I knew it was a toy gun, but Mama Lelethu and her goons didn't know that. It looked very real.

'Enter that gate at your own risk,' my father said while wielding the gun, finger on the trigger. 'I swear you will be transported away from here in a hearse. Come. Just enter that gate if you have a death wish.'

'You must move out. We are giving you until the end of the month, which is a week from now, to vacate.'

'What are you going to do if I don't move out?'

'You must pay rent.'

'Over my dead body. It's my house. Why must I pay rent?' he said.

'It's no longer your house. I bought it.'

'I didn't sell it to you. I have been living here for the past eighteen years. I'm left with only nineteen months to pay off this house. Tell your bank to refund you your damn money.'

Our dog, Milo, watched my father as he shouted. She moved as little of her body as necessary to acknowledge she was awake and guarding our house.

'It's over. Nothing is for free, baba. You must vacate this house. The bank sold it to me because you were unable to pay your bond, remember?'

'Why don't you go and tell the bank to go fuck itself.'

'Here are my papers. Why would the bank sell me the house if it's still yours?'

'That is between you and your damn bank. It is none of my business.'

I watched my father as he stood still, his left hand tensely digging in his right armpit and the other still holding the toy gun. He moved about the veranda with the walk of a victorious wrestler, sweat running along his temples.

A few people were starting to gather along our street. Mama Lelethu and her bodybuilders sensed some trouble coming and decided to walk a few steps towards their car.

'Time will tell. You have to move out by the end of the month.'

'Time is a lie.'

'Maybe a necessary one.'

'Ek phola hierso. I'm going nowhere. Julle plaasjapies cannot threaten me.' His eyes were shining with a fire of greatness and unconquerable courage. The sight of Mama Lelethu and her body-builders was unbearable to him. He was trembling, but I knew it was not from fear; he was trying hard to control himself so as not to do something that he would regret later.

'Very well,' Mama Lelethu said, seeing that my father was not going to budge. 'You are giving me no other choice. You're going to hear from my lawyer. I am going to ask the court for an eviction order – no matter how long it takes or how much it costs. I will have you thrown out.'

She dropped her hands to her sides, and turned away as though turning away from intolerable ugliness.

That afternoon, my father sent me to the nearby hardware store to buy five litres of red paint. He used it to write the following words on our wall:

This house is not for sale.
Buyers and trespassers will be shot in the head.

From that day onwards, our house was known as 'Not for Sale House'. It became a landmark for everyone asking for directions around Protea Glen Extension 11.

Since my father was out of work and afraid of Mama Lelethu's threats, he would sit outside on the veranda every day with his toy gun and a knife. He didn't want her to come back with her bodybuilders to change our door locks. The very notion that such a thing might happen seemed to make him shudder with anger. Every time I came back from school, I would find him half sitting half lying in his rocking chair with his hand in his pocket, a beer bottle and the toy gun on the floor, as he gazed out at the gate. When he saw a car coming, he would straighten his neck, and reach to pick up his toy gun without taking his eyes off the car. As the car passed, he would put the gun down, take off his spectacles, spit on the lenses and wipe the imaginary dust off with the sleeve of his shirt before saying his mantra: 'It's my house. It's not for sale. I will shoot you dead.'

Sometimes tears would stream from his eyes. It was as if he suddenly remembered that if it weren't for the house, he would have nothing and nowhere to go. Some evenings, when he had too much to drink, he imagined shadows passing by the house and would shout: 'This is my house. It's not for sale. I will shoot you dead!'

He also got into the habit of talking to himself, saying the same mantra over and over for hours.

A month passed, but Mama Lelethu did not return and neither did the bodybuilders. We did not hear from her lawyer. It looked as if she was bluffing.

And then, at the end of March, the country went into lockdown due to Covid-19. Very few cars and pedestrians passed by our house and my father started to relax. We did not see or hear anything from Mama Lelethu. She must have been confined somewhere else, unable to get to us.

Before the lockdown, I was doing my grade eleven studies at

Protea Glen Secondary School in Soweto. When the schools closed due to the pandemic, I was supposed to study at home. The teacher sent class work via WhatsApp, but I often didn't have data to download it. I sneaked to my friend Njabulo's house to study.

Despite the stresses Covid brought, it was almost a peaceful time for our family because we again felt secure of our house.

Gradually, restrictions were relaxed and I went back to school. There was still no sign of Mama Lelethu. We started to believe that she had given up.

Then one day Mama Lelethu's lawyer sent a letter to inform us that our eviction case was going to court. The pandemic came to our rescue because the court did not want to evict people during this time. But my parents were disgusted with the bizarre ruling that Mama Lelethu could move into our house with us.

On 21 August, Mama Lelethu rocked up in a white BMW, followed by a bakkie full of her belongings. She was also accompanied by a police sedan. Although she would have preferred us to be gone, moving in with us was more tolerable to Mama Lelethu than losing money by paying for the house she was not living in.

She arrived wearing a very attractive blue dress and blue shoes that were complemented by her blue nail polish. Even the mask covering her nose and mouth was blue. She was a lady of about thirty-six, way younger than my father and mother who were fifty-eight and fifty-three respectively. As she entered through our gate, I caught myself wondering what lotion she used to keep her face looking so healthy. Every curve of her body spoke of beauty and perfection, and her wide, bright eyes smiled at me when I looked at her.

Just like my father, my mother didn't like her from the word go. Our dog, Milo, also didn't like her. The dog even drove her paws into the ground and showed her teeth at our unwelcome visitors. My father, who had been drinking since morning, the ban on the sale of alcohol having been lifted, woke up from his rocking chair to find Milo watching over him with fierce eagerness.

On seeing Mama Lelethu and her entourage coming, my father downed what was left from his glass. There were two police officers, a man and a woman, who got out of the police car. Out of the bakkie climbed the two bodybuilders she had come with previously. There was also another man who got out of the BMW with Mama Lelethu, whom we all assumed was her husband. The man was elegant in a dark suit. Despite having a beard with stray grey hairs, he retained a youthful look.

Mama Lelethu greeted me and my sisters, Asive and Asiphe. With that fancy white BMW, she didn't look like a person desperate for a place to live.

'Someone will die tonight,' my father said, trying to intimidate our unwelcome guests. 'Yes, I can smell some blood in the air.'

'But you agreed that I can live here, too. That's what the court ruled,' said Mama Lelethu. 'Why would you want to kill us now?'

'They forced me into it.'

'Ntate Lebese, your threats are a very serious concern to us,' said the female police officer. 'This person is here because she is the owner of the house and she has a right to live here. The court has confirmed this. You can no longer threaten her. It's over.'

'But this is still my house, and it is not for sale. How do you expect us to live with a complete stranger? She is an unwanted guest.'

'You will have to try to live with her in peace. If you harm her in any way, you will face a long jail sentence. I swear you will not see your family for a very long time if you do something stupid.'

Mama Lelethu and the three men gave no sign of being affected by the threat explicit in my father's words. Maybe it was because the police car was still at the gate. Instead, they started to offload their belongings and move it into our house. The two bodybuilders quietly put the massive fridge next to our small one in the kitchen, as well as a grey microwave next to our little white one. The men radiated a powerful presence, showing off their muscles.

'This is my house. You can't live here,' my father said.

'Please leave them alone,' my mother pleaded. 'We don't want any more trouble. I have had enough.'

For a moment, my father's face remained motionless because of my mother's words. Even when a fly flew up his nose he didn't try to remove it. He was always like that when angry and drunk. He didn't say another word. A few minutes later, his eyes closed and his head nodded forwards. He slumped miserably in the chair. It was not easy to tell whether he was drunk, dozing or eaves-dropping. Beads of sweat trickled down his face. Satisfied that he was suitably subdued, the police officers took their leave and Mama Lelethu's crew continued unpacking.

That night, Mama Lelethu and the three men drank and slept in what used to be my room. On their arrival that afternoon, they had originally started to move their suitcases into my sisters' room. My mother had protested, 'You can't take this room. Where are our daughters going to sleep?'

'Ma Lebese, you are lucky we are only taking one room,' Mama Lelethu had said. 'All of us are cramming in this one room, while this is really my house. I can take all the rooms, if I want. But we are satisfied to share a room. Don't make this difficult.'

They had removed their masks now, feeling at home.

'But my eldest, my daughter Asive, is in her final year at the University of Johannesburg, doing a Communications degree. She needs her room to study. We are looking forward to her graduating this year. She cannot be disturbed. Asive will be the first person in our family to earn a university degree if she passes.'

Mama Lelethu sighed. 'Look, she can stay in this room, and so can your youngest daughter, but we are going to move in. They will be sharing the room with us. All of us. With me and these three men.'

My mother looked at the men with wide eyes. My little sister, Asiphe, was only twelve, and I knew there was no way that my mother was going to allow these strangers to sleep in the same room with her or Asive.

'You can sleep in my room,' I quickly said. 'I will sleep on the couch in the living room.'

'There's a good boy!' Mama Lelethu smiled brilliantly at me and tapped my cheek to show her appreciation.

When they had moved all their luggage into my room, the four of them shut themselves inside it.

At first, they were considerate with the noise they were making, except when opening the door to go to our only toilet. Sometimes, when the toilet was occupied, the men would go outside to pee and to smoke while wearing only their boxer shorts. It seemed that they never smoked inside the room. On three occasions, one of the two bodybuilders, the one with huge, drooped lips, came out of the house to smoke his joint.

Around midnight, I was still in the sitting room with my mother and sisters. My father was sleeping in the master bedroom. But we did not feel like going to bed and could not imagine sleeping with the strangers under our roof. Only Asiphe eventually dozed off with her head on our mother's shoulder.

It was then that we heard some weird sounds from the strangers' room. Asive and I went and pressed our ears to the unwelcome guests' door and listened. There was a sharp moaning. It got louder and louder until the woman sounded like she was out of breath. My sister and I tiptoed back to the couch where our mother was sitting, pretending to be watching television.

'That's it. They are watching porn movies, Mom,' Asive whispered. 'I told you these guys are freaks.'

'Was it the real stuff or just a movie scene?' I wondered.

'I swear it was a porn movie. The lady was moaning in English with background music.'

My mother could hardly hide her disgust. 'What kind of people are they?' she hissed, raising her eyebrows. 'One woman has three men in our house. I have never seen anything like this before in my life. We can't allow this woman to turn our house into a brothel. This has to stop. Your father or the court must do something.'

'I told you that I saw her carrying sexual objects in a box when they were offloading stuff,' Asive said. 'I saw a dildo, handcuffs and vibrators.'

'Stop it, Asive,' our mother said, checking to see that her youngest

16

was still asleep and oblivious to this talk. 'Where do you know those things from?'

'But, Ma, who doesn't know a dildo in this day and age? I mean, it is everywhere. You can even buy it at the Pakistani spaza shop down the road.'

'That's it. I can't deal with this any more. These people will ruin my children.'

My mother got up, irritated, waking Asiphe in the process. Ma stomped off and ducked inside the master bedroom where my father was snoring, slamming the door behind her. Asiphe was still half asleep and Asive also decided to go to bed, so they disappeared to their bedroom. I switched off the light and the television, then looked at the time on my cellphone screen. It was fourteen minutes to one in the morning. There were still noises coming from my bedroom with mbaqanga music playing in the background. I lay there listening to it in the dark, unable to fall asleep.

Minutes later, someone switched on the sitting-room lights. When I was no longer blinded by the sudden brightness, I saw my father standing by our unwelcome guests' room, awake and seemingly sober. After rubbing his face with his hand, he knocked at their door.

'Who's there?' a male voice came from inside the room.

'People are sleeping, you must switch that thing off and stop talking. It is late at night and we are trying to sleep.'

One of the bodybuilders opened the room wearing only his boxer shorts. His lips moved constantly, as if experimenting with irreverent grins, grimaces and sneers. 'Who are you to tell us to switch our TV off? We are watching a movie here. Please don't disturb us.'

'Let me speak to the lady, not you. I have no good words to say to you.'

I felt a surge of unreasonable hatred towards the man. Who was he to speak so condescendingly to my father?

Mama Lelethu appeared. 'Baba Lebese, I know we are not your favourite people. But please try to be reasonable. We are adults and not your children. Your hatred will pass. When we've been here for weeks and months, you'll soon get used to our sight and end up liking us. Believe me, you will. In the meantime, you can join us if you want to. We are having drinks. Would you like a whisky or a beer?'

For a moment I thought my father would give in to Mama Lelethu's bewitching smile. But their eyes met in naked hatred.

'I don't want to have your drink. I want you to switch your damn TV off. We are trying to sleep. Just because the court said you can come into this house doesn't mean you can open a brothel here.' He made an obscene gesture with his two fingers. 'Or did you also tell the court that you're a prostitute and that you would be bringing men to have sex in my house?'

Mama Lelethu sniffed, and took her time answering. Her eyes darted anxiously to the right and left. 'Look here, old man, first of all, you can never call me a prostitute again. Who I bring home or have sex with is none of your goddamn business.'

'You made it my business when you came into my house, which is not a brothel.'

'As far as I remember, you do not have the title deed to this house – but I do. I also don't remember signing a lease agreement with you. This means we can have a braai or a party anytime, anywhere on the property, including in the living area. We can even invite anyone we want to.'

'You don't …' He could not even finish his sentence.

'Fuck off out of my face.'

My father's hand pressed against his open mouth. He slowly retreated, as if being pushed back by an invisible but irresistible force. Mama Lelethu slammed her door shut. I saw my father raise his fist as if to bang on the door, but he restrained himself. I guessed there was nothing he could do to her out of respect for the court and fear of the bodybuilders. Shaking his head and looking disgusted, he walked away. He passed the couch where I pretended to be sleeping. He then crept silently to the smaller couch, found his jacket that was lying there, and shook it to remove every trace of imaginary fluff. While facing the front door, he put the jacket over his shoulders. The light bulb above flung his shadow towards the door, ahead of him. With a few quick steps, he seized the knob, flung open the door, exited and slammed it with a mighty crash behind him. The force shook the windowpanes.

A minute later, my mother came into the sitting room. She gripped the curtains with both hands as she peered out to where our father was heading. I got up and went to stand next to her, to get a peek. A ghostly light from the street lamp lay in a long shaft from our window into the street. My father was walking in the direction of the Shell garage. My mother startled as I coughed beside her. She threw a frightened glance at what used to be my bedroom.

'Mbongisi, what did that woman say to your father to make him so upset?'

'I don't know, Ma. I was asleep,' I lied.

'One day life will catch up with her and she'll have to answer for everything she's done.'

I couldn't sleep for the remainder of the morning hours. The mbaqanga music that our unwelcome guests were playing disturbed that sleep-inducing part of my brain. Useless thoughts crowded my head. My heart was beating as if waiting for something. There was a perpetual noise in my ears, and I often involuntarily raised my hand while lying on the couch. Eventually I tiptoed to our unwelcome guests' bedroom door and stuck my ear against it to listen.

'Maybe he has gone to the police station to report us.' It was a male voice that sounded like the bodybuilder who had been talking to my father earlier. 'He will be disappointed that we have our people in the police force, too.'

'Waste of time. No one will take him seriously. Your boss, Mrs Zungu, solved that part. I'm glad I went to her for help with this matter of my house. I need to call her in the morning to let her know of our progress. I hope these people will soon leave,' said Mama Lelethu. 'I'm getting fed up now.'

'Don't worry, Mrs Zungu's plan to throw a house party every weekend is going to work. That will make them leave soon,' a male voice said.

'Certainly. Their children still go to school and exams are coming up. No parent would like their children to be disturbed by our noise. They don't know what is coming for them,' Mama Lelethu said, and they all laughed.

'Mrs Zungu always says that the legal route of eviction is just a waste of time and money,' another male voice said. 'Now with Covid, even more so. We are her trusted team when it comes to these matters of evicting people our black way. She will be happy with our progress so far.'

There was a pause, then, a male voice:

'I have an idea.'

'Let's hear it. What do you have in mind, Stix?' one of the men said.

'Well, it is similar to what we did in Midrand to that woman who refused to move out. How about we invite a few dirty-looking nyaope addicts to the party tomorrow? We will play loud music and let them dance in the yard. I tell you that these people will be annoyed more than they are annoyed with us now. Trust me, they will leave soon.'

'I agree with Stix. That will be the final nail in their coffin. We can even burn impepho any moment we want, or cook our tripe without having washed it so that there are flies everywhere inside the house.'

It all sounded very bizarre. The men who had come with Mama Lelethu were in the employ of some woman called Mrs Zungu who seemed to specialise in terrorising people out of their houses. To prove to myself that I was not dreaming or sleepwalking, I had to pinch my hand. That really convinced me that I was awake and in full possession of my senses.

It was now clear that my parents were fighting a losing battle. Our unwelcome guests were planning to do everything in their power to make themselves permanently intolerable to us.

The light click of the snapping lock inside my mother's bedroom brought me round, as if from a spell of unconsciousness. I went back to the couch and lay down. I could hear the rats as they played above the ceiling. One rat squealed and struggled up there. The ceiling shook a bit. Fortunately, I caught some sleep.

In the morning, my father was still not home. My mother, Asive, Asiphe and I were on our way to the Protea Police Station. The township sky looked dirty. As it normally does in Soweto around this time, the wind was blowing from all four corners of the township and from every side of the street. That fierce wind appeared to have pruned the trees so savagely overnight that they looked humiliated and punished for having green leaves and shade in spring and summertime. A number of satellite dishes attached to the nearby block of flats looked like giant dirty mushrooms because of the red dust that covered them.

A dazzling sun was already creating mirages on the tarmac as we approached the police station in a minibus taxi.

Inside the police station, a policewoman asked, 'Who is next?', while looking at us. 'For affidavits, you must go to that counter there.' She pointed with her finger. 'If you want to report a case, come to this desk. All the police vans are out. If your matter is very urgent you will have to wait for the next available police car.'

The policewoman was a very dark, fat lady. The black mask she was wearing had slipped off her nose and only covered her mouth. My mother, sisters and I approached her desk.

'We are here to report a case of abuse,' my mother told her.

'What's wrong, Mama? Is your husband abusing you and your

children? If you want to report him for maintenance, just write on that affidavit.'

'No, it's not my husband who is abusing us. My husband is also a victim of abuse from the people we are living with in our house.'

'Your tenants? What did they do to you, Mama? If they are trouble, you must give them notice to vacate your house.'

'They are not necessarily our tenants. The court put them there. But we can't live with those people. They play porn movies so loudly until the morning. That woman lives with three men in one room inside our house.'

Everyone inside the police station looked at us. My sisters and I were embarrassed. The police officer rolled up the whites of her eyes. It was an obvious sign that she didn't trust what my mother was saying to her. She paused, and I thought she was going to probe my mother some more. Instead, she burst out in uproarious laughter. The top half of her mouth was now also visible above her mask.

'Are you sure about that, Mama? Besides, adult people watch porn movies all the time. It's not necessarily a crime.'

'But my children are in the same house with that woman and her sex addiction every night, including my twelve-year-old.' She pointed at Asiphe.

'Mama, I'm just saying we need a proper reason to come and talk to those people to tone it down. Does she watch these porn movies with your children, perhaps? Or is it child porn that she is watching? At least that is a serious crime.'

'No, but our house is now turned into a brothel with those three men who stay with her in the room.'

The officer laughed again. She then prodded her female colleague next to her, making her head twitch like a horse having its teeth inspected. The other officer looked at us, shaking to keep her mirth inside. They were condescending, but my mother hardly realised it.

'Are you sure about the brothel thing, Mama?' the first officer continued as her colleague started to laugh out loud. 'Just because there are three men doesn't mean they are paying her. They might just enjoy her . . . company.'

'Well, we heard some sexual moans and groans in there from the TV and it disturbs my children,' my mother said. 'They are about to write exams at their schools.'

'Let me get this straight . . .' The officer seemed to be enjoying probing my mother. 'Does this lady watch porn inside her room?'

'Yes. And our rooms are in the same house. My son here sleeps in the living room.'

'How often does she watch this porn?'

'Well, she watched until the early hours of this morning.'

'Whose house is it?'

'Well, it was our house until the bank auctioned it and sold it to her illegally.'

'So, it is basically her house and you're her tenants?' she said, then touched her right ear mechanically and frowned.

'Well, according to the bank, yes, but we have not been evicted by the court.'

'But, Mama, what she does in her private space is none of the police's business. People can privately watch porn, including you and your husband.'

'I don't want my children, especially my girls, to live in permanent terror of having to go to bed in a house full of strange men
and a woman who watch porn movies.'

'I will tell you this. I will file your complaint, and when the police
vans arrive, I will send them to come and investigate, okay? But
I don't think they will see your complaint as urgent.'

My mother was furious when we left the police station. I didn't
know how to tell her about the conversation that I'd eavesdropped
on that morning.

When we arrived home, there was a police sedan parked outside.

'Didn't that woman say that there was no police car available?'
my mother asked suspiciously. 'I knew she was lying.'

'Maybe they just didn't want to give us a lift home, Mama,' said
Asive.

Two police officers were inspecting the wheels of Mama Lelethu's BMW while taking statements from our unwelcome guests.
The car looked dirty, a thin film of dust covering it all over.

'Ah, here you are, Mrs Lebese. We are looking for your husband.'

'My husband? What happened to him? Is everything okay?'

'You tell us. We are investigating a matter of malicious damage
to property. Your husband is the prime suspect so far. Miss Nala
here woke up this morning to find her two front tyres flat after being
slashed by a knife.'

'Did she say it was my husband's knife?'

'That's what we are investigating, and your husband will help
us with this investigation. So far we are looking at the evidence of
a footprint that we found.'

'So, in this township dust you still found a footprint? Are you sure it was that of my husband?'

'We also hope it's not him. But in view of what they tell us about how he threatened them yesterday, it all points in his direction. His obstinacy in occupying this house while it has been sold to Miss Nala will make us lose all inclination to speak up on his behalf.'

My mother shook her head. She appeared overcome by fear – a fear of violence, of destruction, of the end of the world. She was shaking a bit and looked like she was feverish. At the same time, Mama Lelethu cast some furtive, apologetic looks our way. She had no makeup on, just plain good looks handed down by the gods. Only a small scar under her left eye was unworthy of her admirable face and body.

'Well, I don't know where he is since he left in the early hours of the morning,' my mother said to the police officer. 'He will have to speak for himself.'

'Here is my card. Please tell him to report to the police station when he comes back.'

This seemed to be in accord with Mama Lelethu's most fervent desires and expectations. She thanked the police before they drove away.

Then Mama Lelethu addressed my mother: 'I don't have a problem with you, Mrs Lebese. I can tell you're a very nice person. The problem is your husband. It seems he hates me for no particular reason. His mouth is two steps ahead of his head when he speaks to me. He insulted me in the early hours of the morning by calling me a prostitute. I suspect he slashed my tyres, as you can see.'

'Are you saying what is really in your heart and mind, or are you repeating what the police told you?'

'I'm being honest with you. I can see you are a peaceful person, just like me.'

For the first time, I realised that Mama Lelethu was chewing gum. She turned her head, took off her mask, and spat the gum on the ground.

'I will ask to talk to him,' my mother replied in a detached tone. 'But I don't believe he did it. This place is full of young criminals who are also nyaope addicts.'

'Please talk to him. We don't need to fight. We cannot afford to be petty people who take our grievances to ridiculous levels like this. I know it's difficult, but some people you just have to embrace, in one way or another, for the sake of coexistence. Even if you don't like them or what they do, you have to bite your tongue to remain sane in their company. We can't afford to be sad every time we see each other. Sadness is very close to hate, Mrs Lebese.'

'I hear you well. But tell me this: did all three of those men really sleep in your room at the same time last night?'

'Of course, yes. Where else would they sleep? You don't want them to sleep in the rooms that you or your daughters still occupy.'

'Well, is one of them your husband?'

'Let me just say to you that commitment to one person is imprisonment, Mrs Lebese. Don't you think?'

'Oh ... I thought you were married?'

'Me, married? No way. I cannot accept the subservient position that always happens to a woman in marriage.'

'I don't mean to intrude in your life. I just want to know the person we are living with better . . . So it is true that they are all your men?'

'Well, I don't think that is relevant. But all I can say is that I didn't leave my husband for a life of freedom and adventure to end up chained to one person's desires.'

'But three at the same time, kodwa?'

'Life is an adventure to be embraced with an open mind and loving heart, my dear sister,' she said. 'I always wanted something out of the ordinary.'

'All right, it's your choice.'

'Definitely it is. But listen here, we will be having a braai this afternoon. Don't be surprised to hear music and see my friends arriving. You can join us if you want to. It's a housewarming party my friends have organised for me,' she said with what sounded like false modesty.

'Maybe next time, but not today. My children have to study. They have exams coming soon. And I have to clean the house.'

'Well, I hope you will all get used to the sight of me in this house, and maybe we will end up liking each other.'

That afternoon, the smell of braai meat and the sound of house music and people laughing and talking drifted in from the yard. My mother warned us to stay indoors and not to attend the braai outside. She told us that my father would be very upset if he found us outside mingling with our unwelcome guests. My sisters and I agreed, but deep down I wanted to join the festivities. I couldn't help but move my jaw several times at the smell of the braai meat outside.

In the kitchen, the aroma of the fresh bread that had just been delivered by the bakery guy for the party drifted to me. I was immediately hungry. I peeked at the plate inside our microwave and fingered yesterday's pap and cabbage. The pap looked hard and flat and difficult to force down.

I could not concentrate because of the clatter of knives, forks and plates that took the place of the conversation outside for a while. I was also absorbed by the house music that our unwelcome guests were playing. The melody was so captivating that even Asiphe hummed and mumbled the words from inside her bedroom. Outside, many of the guests who had by now finished eating were drinking, dancing or singing off-tune.

That mental disassociation from the events of the day outside was torturous. I stayed in the sitting room pretending to be reading and watching TV at the same time. The truth is, I was in fact sniffing the aromas that came wafting in through the kitchen window.

I went and stood by the window, secretly surveying Mama Lelethu and her female friends as they danced and gyrated in circles.

I felt like I was an outcast from life's big feast.

There was a steady stream of people coming in and out of our house as they wanted to use our only toilet. My mother expressed her annoyance to them or whispered curses. She complained to the ladies that she had just scraped away hardened faecal matter from the toilet bowl, just to embarrass them. She pleaded with the males that they must point straight at the bowl when taking a pee instead of peeing on the floor that had just been mopped. In the meantime, she disinfected everything that she believed came into contact with human waste inside the house.

She was now cleaning the wall next to the stove which she thought our unwelcome guests had deliberately blackened with smoke. She seemed reduced to absolute despair. She sniffed at the unwashed pot on the stove and then moved away with an expression of disgust. She complained that my former room was now cramped and dark, and that it smelled of marijuana, leftover food and coffee, which had already attracted cockroaches to our house. She opened Mama Lelethu's microwave, and the sight of a heap of clean bones inside it made her look away in disgust.

'This is not life,' she said to herself, as if wondering if there were people who could stand more pain than her. 'I can't do this any more.'

My father returned when the evening was drawing to a close, bringing the darkness with him, and a strong smell of alcohol and tobacco. As he entered through the gate, attention shifted to him like waves being pulled by the moon. Even our dog, Milo, lolled her tongue from a happy face as if welcoming him. My mother sprung to her feet and raced out of the living room when she spotted him through the window. She probably didn't want him to cause a scene, as he seemed drunk.

Our unwelcome guests remained seated when he passed by with my mother.

'What's happening in my house?' he asked.

'Where have you been?' my mother countered while helping him to get inside the house. 'The police were looking all over for you.'

'The police? What for? I needed some fresh air, so I just walked around the township. Why were they looking for me?'

'Did you do it? Did you slash their car tyres?'

'Whose car tyres? The police? No.'

'I mean that car outside?'

'Oh, that one.' He pointed at Mama Lelethu's car outside, not only with no expression of surprise, but with an air of indifference. 'Even if it were me, those bastards deserve it. Whoever did it is my hero.'

My mother responded with muttered, harsh words. She looked nervous and started blinking rapidly. She twisted my father's arm a bit. 'Did you do it, Mfundo?' my mother shouted at him.

'The bastards deserve it. Who do they think they are to make a noise in my house? I'm going outside to chase them away now,' he said as he took a few drunken steps towards the door.

'You can't keep behaving like this. Let them do what they have to do. Don't put our lives and yours in danger.'

He had to be stopped, calmed, convinced and finally won over by my mother. She then made him sit on the couch, and pressed herself up against him, an arm around his neck. It looked more like she was strangling him than a sign of affection.

'I'm tired of fighting, Mfundo. Just leave them alone.'

'As long as they respect the fact that this is still my house. We have rules in this house. But for now I will leave them as you ask me to.'

'If this dream of yours about getting this house back still makes sense to you after you have woken up, maybe that is because you have not woken up yet. This is no longer our house, Mfundo.'

'This is my house. Everyone knows that. It is not for sale.'

My mother's endurance looked like it was draining away. She

stood up and looked at my father. 'I need peace and quiet, Mfundo, where no one will drive me to the brink of despair. I don't care if it's in the squatter camp or a hostel or a village.'

The nodding of my father's drunken head showed that he was not far from dozing off. My mother gave him a quick hug but did not hold him tight. She stood up and he slumped down onto the couch, and it looked as though he was finally settling in to his regular drunken evening snooze. Within a few minutes, he was asleep, breathing through his mouth as he always did after drinking, awake or asleep.

'Tomorrow I'm leaving this place, with or without you, Mfundo. I can't live in this house any more. We are like ghosts with no faces.'

As my exams approached two months later, my parents often let me study and sleep at my friend Njabulo's house because I could not concentrate at home where my privacy was violated every day by our unwelcome guests. What used to be our home had become a place of alienation and fights. We had experienced the strangers' wrath, their unreasonableness, and general inconsiderateness towards us with their late-night noises and unnecessary parties. Despite all this, my mother had not left the house, even though she threatened to go away almost every day.

Njabulo and I were studying with another friend, Sabelo, and watching TV at Njabulo's home when a thought came to my mind. There was a programme on TV that showed a Halloween costume party and children trick-or-treating in their costumes. They were dressed as skeletons, ghosts and scary witches. It was mid-October and American shows were starting to focus on Halloween.

'This Halloween is a waste of pumpkins,' Sabelo said.

'I don't believe in this American thing,' Njabulo agreed. 'In fact, I don't care about it. Let's change the programme, guys.'

'No, wait! This is it, guys,' I said. 'We must get costumes like these tomorrow.'

'What for?' Njabulo looked at me like I was crazy. 'Nobody trick-or-treats here. And anyway, it's not Halloween yet. That's kids' stuff, man.'

'Listen,' I pleaded, 'I have a good idea. I think it will help to get rid of our guests at home.' I shared my plan with them. I found it so funny that I burst out laughing as I explained it to them.

'What if they shoot at us?' asked Njabulo.

'I don't think they have a gun. Otherwise they would have shot my father a long time ago.'

'Count me in,' said Sabelo. 'You must get your room back, my friend.'

The following day, the three of us went to the China Mall along the Main Reef Road. Njabulo, who had now fallen in love with the idea, used his money to buy a Halloween costume of a were-wolf. The hairy suit would cover the whole body of the person who'd wear it and there was a mask, too, which fitted over your head. The mask had a snout and open mouth with big, fanged teeth. Njabulo didn't have enough money for any other costumes, but he could buy two sets of glow-in-the-dark vampire teeth. We agreed to wait until a rainy night to pull off our prank, for maximum scary effect.

On the Friday night after writing our last exam, the sky emptied itself in a terrible downpour. The pale moonlight covered the township with a ghostly glow. Sabelo, Njabulo and I decided this was the day. Njabulo suggested that we buy a live chicken and four candles made of black wax for our plan. We then waited until it was the early hours of the morning when everyone was asleep.

The rain had abated for about an hour. The three of us went to my home. There was no one in the wet streets. Njabulo was dressed in the werewolf costume since he was the one who'd bought it. I wanted to argue that I should wear it, since it was my plan, but I didn't want anything to jeopardise our mission now. Njabulo could refuse to take part or take back his costume. Sabelo and I had the vampire teeth in our mouths.

Sabelo was carrying a live chicken. When we arrived at our home, he slaughtered the chicken and let the blood drip on the roof of Mama Lelethu's car. We then stood by Mama Lelethu's window with the three burning candles. I knew how to open the window from outside due to a broken latch, and had done it many times before when this was still my bedroom. I knocked at the window first before I opened it and waited in the dark.

As soon as Mama Lelethu and one of the bodybuilders peeped through the open window, there was a scream. They simultaneously lifted up their arms to cover their sleepy faces.

Njabulo nudged me to put the candles near his face. It lit up his grey werewolf face with the long, sharp teeth. He pushed aside the curtains and did his rehearsed roar. This terrified our unwelcome guests and they fell over themselves to get away. Mama Lelethu ran into the side of the bed in her haste and toppled over its corner, landing heavily on the floor on the far side of the bed.

She lay cowering and whimpering. One of the bodybuilders had jerked the door open so violently in an attempt to get out of the room that it had sprung open suddenly and knocked him in the head. He collapsed, his dead weight slamming the door shut. With him passed out in front of the closed door, the other two men struggled to get out, to no avail. They started to drag his body, half-naked and only in his boxer shorts, out of the way. We managed to restrain ourselves from laughing, and silently hurried out of our yard. The dead chicken we left on top of Mama Lelethu's car.

The following morning when I got home, I found the police there. One of them was putting the dead chicken into a plastic bag as evidence. Both my parents were standing there, together with my sisters, the two bodybuilders, the well-dressed gentleman and Mama Lelethu. She looked terrified.

'Are you sure you were not drunk or something?' asked the officer.

'What do you mean? I'm sure it was some wild overgrown creatures. Probably a pack of baboons. I saw the large hairy one clearly. The other two, I just saw the terrible sharp teeth. That's why I woke Ntate Lebese up from the other room as soon as we could get out. It must have killed this chicken and left it here.'

'Do we have baboons or wild animals in this area? Maybe it's the nyaope addicts who were trying to scare you.'

'Not a chance. Those ones would have preferred to roast the chicken rather than leave it on the car with blood all over,' said one bodybuilder. 'I also saw them. It's exactly as Lelethu described. The creatures all had long, sharp teeth. But I think they were on fire too – I saw flames.'

'Those sound like creatures out of hell,' the officer remarked dryly.

'I'm not surprised,' my mother said and everyone looked at her. 'This house has been haunted. They once found the body of the previous owner next to that corner of the wall. It seemed he had been eaten by rats. Now that you mention the creatures and the sharp teeth, it makes a lot of sense.'

'You have seen them, too?'

'A couple of times. Just fleetingly. That's why I use my snuff to communicate with my ancestors every night before I sleep.' My mother nodded absentmindedly.

'What do you mean? Do you think there is witchcraft involved?'

'I mean, where have you seen a baboon in Soweto? These are not baboons; these are the ghosts of the past visiting this place. We live in a haunted house. These spirits will sacrifice some of us one day.'

Mama Lelethu's eyes started to beg for an explanation that my father didn't have. She made a gagging sound as if someone were strangling her. 'What do you mean the spirits will sacrifice us one day?' she asked with flaring nostrils. 'So you guys knew this all along?'

'Yes. It's a pity you didn't ask us. We would have told you,' my mother said.

'You should have warned us,' Mama Lelethu said sharply. She put a shaky hand to her head.

My father shrugged his shoulders in reply, which was his easy way out of explaining things.

For the next few weeks, our unwelcome guests slept with their lights on. They also didn't spend a lot of nights at home, which was wonderful for my parents. Mama Lelethu was overtaken with attacks of asthma that left her gasping for breath after our prank. She woke up wheezing and heaving for breath in the early hours of the morning.

But as the weeks passed without incident, Mama Lelethu and her crew started to gain courage. I overheard them wondering if what they'd seen had been real or a trick played on them.

'After all, this family will probably do anything to scare us out of their house.'

'Yes, and where was the boy on the night that it happened? He could be involved.'

When I told my friends about this conversation, they agreed that we had to play some tricks on our unwelcome guests again. We picked another night when the rain pelted heavily for the deed. Sabelo and Njabulo enlisted another one of our friends, Senzo, to help them. They agreed that I must remain inside our house this time.

Njabulo had bought an ugly ebony doll and put some oil on its navel. He, Sabelo and Senzo had then pinned needles all over the doll's body. That night, they dressed up again and threw it through the window into Mama Lelethu's room.

I was in the sitting room, pretending to sleep, but I knew the exact moment the doll landed in Mama Lelethu's room because she screamed so loudly and ran out to where I pretended to be awakened by her shouts. She was followed by the three men. They peered at the front door but seemed too afraid to venture outside.

'They are back. This time they threw a voodoo doll at me. Please help me!' Mama Lelethu choked out, wringing her hands in my direction.

'What is happening now?' my father asked, coming from his bedroom. He sounded irritated. My mother trailed behind him and my sisters poked their heads out of their own bedroom.

'The spirits,' she said, pointing to her room. 'The same ones that came the last time. Or witches in the form of beasts. Whatever they are . . .'

'Please go back to sleep and close your windows,' my father growled. 'Why are these spirits or witches only visiting you anyway?'

'You don't believe me? I saw smoke and flames shoot out of our window. Go in there and you will see what they have thrown at me.'

Everyone gathered in the living room as my father went inside their bedroom. He quickly came out again, looking very concerned.

'I think you guys need some cleansing. It seems you are being followed by strange and evil things.'

My family members retreated to the safety of their respective rooms.

Mama Lelethu, her male companions and I could not sleep for the remainder of the morning. They had made beds for themselves in the living room, too afraid to go back into their bedroom. Mama Lelethu's teeth clattered with fear.

Having calmed down a little, one of the men suggested, 'It could still be someone trying to trick us . . .'

'Who?' Mama Lelethu demanded. 'Every member of the Lebese family was inside when it happened.'

'They could have hired someone.' I could feel the man staring at me even though I had my eyes closed, feigning sleep.

'The father did not look as if he knew anything about it. He was scared when he saw that doll.'

'How can spirits throw a doll?'

'How must I know, but we saw it happen. It must be witchcraft. Those must have been witches in the form of baboons.'

They were silent for a while. Then I recognised the sound of rats in the roof. They had frequented this part of the living-room ceiling before, but I hadn't heard them lately.

'Do you hear that?' Mama Lelethu whispered in a panicked voice. 'They are inside the house!' The clawing and bumping was magnified by the early-morning silence. I opened my eyes and saw she had jumped up and was staring at me and the three men in stark, stupid cowardice.

Just then, we heard a tearing noise and a big, fat rat fell from above, landing at Mama Lelethu's feet. She screamed in terror as two more rats, slightly smaller, rained down on her.

I looked up. A smallish hole had torn in the ceiling, probably worn away by the rats over time.

'The rats! They've sent the rats to eat me alive!' she yelled as she stormed out the front door. If she had not been engulfed by fear, she might have noticed the beautiful sunrise.

The men, all three of them, did not waste time in running after her, deadly afraid of what those rats would do. I had a feeling they were not coming back.

I shook my head and laughed as my family members appeared to check on the commotion. Whoever knew I would be grateful to a bunch of rats?

MY LOVER'S SECRET

Gina, I assume you're wondering why I'm writing to you now after almost a year has passed since those few months we spent living together. I'm still here in Houghton, Johannesburg, in the same house we shared during that time. The place where you wrote your now bestselling novel. And that's why I'm writing: to congratulate you on its release. But you might suspect me of wanting to say more, and maybe you're right.

Just like I told you before, whenever I read any of your books, it seems that my whole history is summarised within them. But your recent offering in particular made me recall my long history of imposed silence. I told you when we were still together that I was once muted. During that time, I read constantly and kept to myself.

Now I've read your new book. It revealed the secrets that I had kept in some abandoned drawer of my brain for years. Those secrets often reappeared in the fantastical form of a dream.

Where do I even begin? Yes, my void. As I once shared with you, my memory of my childhood is full of holes. Meeting you was cathartic. You were like an angel sent to help me. Before you, there was only the void with no beginning and no end. Then I met you. Your vision and mental landscape seemed to be the same as mine. Just like yours, my world had been constructed as inferior to that of men. But you broke free, and so did I.

Just so that you know, that day in March was not the first time that I met you. You have been in my life since I read your first book, *Sisterhood*, and started a book club named after it. It felt like you had taken me into your private world and revealed yourself to me.

The Sisterhood Book Club bought and read all three of your subsequent books. You won't believe this, but I made posters of your fourth book, *Men for Hire*, to display in my house. I pasted it all over my library wall. What a title, I thought. I remember buying twenty-five copies one day at The Bookstore. I gave them to friends and members of my book club to read. Oh, what a story! The Sisterhood Book Club must have discussed it about five times since it came out. It resonated with my life.

When I finished reading it the first time, I knew that my own link to my family was abruptly broken. I have not seen my family for the past two years, although they don't live far from my address. It's about twenty-seven kilometres from here. But like you warned in *Men for Hire*, kinship does not automatically exist between people who have fed from the same breast. The book showed me that my feeling of isolation and separation had been caused by my trauma. I was so profoundly happy that I'd discovered it.

Over the years I attended some of your launches and readings, and you even signed some of my books, but there was no deep conversation until that day at the launch of *Men for Hire* at Hyde Park Corner. I know you don't remember the previous meetings, but surely you remember the time at Hyde Park? Let me remind you. I was not going to miss the launch of *Men for Hire* for anything in this world. I even cancelled my shift at the hospital just to come to hear you speak. During your launch, I just sat there and watched you as you moved your eyes from one person to the next. You occasionally smiled at me when answering the questions from the audience. Or maybe that's what I thought you did. You read my favourite chapter of your book slowly. You watched carefully where the commas fell so that you could convey the natural pauses. I was salivating. That passage you read invoked my past of rupture and loss. It revealed my fractured identity. The damaged main character of that tale was so like me. Later that night, my past returned to me in the form of intrusive questions. Unpleasant ideas, unpleasant truths came to my consciousness again. I think it was due to my extreme anxiety and shame about my past.

At the launch, you smiled at every woman, even at the objects like the microphones and water jugs in the room. Those of us who are usually unseen became suddenly visible. I've never seen a room so full of black women as the space where your launch was held. It was like I was in a classroom where every girl swooned over their crush – you. I felt like walking across the room and touching you. As if that was a way for me to regain the sanity I think I lost a long time ago.

What a charmer you are. You made us all applaud when you told the audience that, after your divorce, you had to undergo a psychological cleansing from the oppression of men. People applauded spontaneously.

The question asked by that man in the navy suit was meaningless, ridiculous, ironic and absurd. 'Are you an angry black woman?'

What nonsense was that? I don't even know why he was there

in the first place. Ninety-nine per cent of the audience was women. Why did his lady drag him along? I think he embarrassed her with that question. He spoke his English out of his nose as if a sneeze were trapped in there. But you answered him gently.

I still remember what you told him. First, you sat with only one buttock on your chair as if you might fart in public out of sheer disgust. You took your time in answering, and drank water from the plastic bottle on the table in front of you. 'My book seeks to reconstruct, recover and understand black women's experiences with patriarchy and marriage by taking into account gender construction and the impact thereof,' you said. 'Men like you can see their own individual and collective interests officially recognised by patriarchy, validated and represented in society. We as women have to struggle even to open our mouths.'

There was rapturous applause from us, your fans.

After the discussion, my book club members and I stood quietly in a corner enjoying the wine and snacks that were served to the noisy room. Everyone was waiting for a chance to talk to you. We wanted to let you know that our club's name had been inspired by your debut book. The Sisterhood Book Club consists of professional women, mostly unmarried, divorced, estranged and separated. I personally wanted to let you know that I had read all four of your books and could relate to your characters' experiences at the hands of men and their repression by the patriarchy. I felt like you were someone just like me, as if moulded by my own family and community. But how could I tell you such sensitive information with the crescendo of chattering voices and clinking glasses that permeated the room?

I finally got a chance to greet you and introduced myself, your number-one fan. You had a smooth, shining face and an expression of permanent delight. You gave me so much undivided attention. You listened carefully when I told you how I formed our women-only book club. You were curious to know more about it. I told you we indulged in massages, facials, saunas and drinking wine while talking books. I then invited you to do a reading at our book club and of course offered to pay you for your time. To my surprise, you said yes immediately. Were you just trying to get my phone number, saying you would check your calendar and let me know when you were free?

After all, that night you called and invited me for drinks at your hotel, The Capital on Bath. I knew right then that you had the same feeling for me that I had for you. We sat until the hotel restaurant was empty, talking and drinking.

'I've been following your writing since your first book,' I said to you.

'Really? Your face looks very familiar,' you said, smiling. 'I think I've seen you in my dreams.'

I was charmed by your supernumerary teeth in your upper jaw when you smiled. Your mouth looked beautifully overcrowded by the teeth that pushed forwards.

'I've been to most of your Joburg readings and launches. Last year I even flew to Cape Town just to attend the festival where you were invited.'

'Why would you do that to yourself?' you asked jokingly.

'I think it's because reading your books and listening to you speak is an act of repairing the harm caused by my family.'

'I'm honoured to hear that. Some clever people say that books are windows to the soul. Now I believe them.'

You agreed to come to my house in Houghton for dinner the following day. You were impressed to see my personal library full of books. You were equally surprised to see so many of your own books – I had bought ten copies of each title, which I asked you to sign.

'Why so many copies? Are you selling them?' you asked.

'Actually, I don't know why I bought so many. But I often give your books as gifts. I think your books healed my pain of coming from the margin as a black woman who is not married. Your writing has opened a secret doorway, and with it I feel I have the key to life. I want to give that key to others as well.'

'Thank you,' you said. 'But be careful of overvaluing my writing and thoughts.'

That's when I confided in you about my personal life, and my relationship with my mother, which had not been good. There had only been politeness, but no real love. And sometimes there was even suppressed indignation at having been forced to be a family at all. I had told her things that had happened to me as a girl, but she did not want to listen. I knew from an early age that not all family members can be trusted. The pain gets too much, especially when your own mother pretends like you don't exist. It is like you are dead.

As I got older, every time she was angry, she used to tell me that 'God may give you everything but not a husband'. As if I were being punished for being wicked. As if, in turn, I were punishing her with my lack of a husband.

'A husband – that word efficiently expresses the pain of patriarchy to me too,' you said. 'I was once trapped in that horrible institution.'

'Oh yes, I heard that you are divorced. I'm sorry it didn't work out between you and your ex-husband.'

'I'm actually happy about it,' you said. 'Marriage is one of the biggest lies of our civilisation. It is the most overrated institution.' You looked at me. 'How about you? Have you been married before?'

'I have never been married. Not even once. That's part of the reason I'm afraid of going home.'

'Why is that, if I may ask? Please forgive my intrusion into your private life. And please don't answer if the question makes you uncomfortable.'

'Don't worry. For me the question is therapeutic. Where do I start? Let me say that during my family meetings, the same question of when I'm going to be married is often asked. It irritates me. My mother always spoke of my beauty to men as if I did not deserve to be without a husband.'

'I'm sorry to hear that,' you said and continued to chew each mouthful of your dinner slowly as if you wanted to savour it. 'Women should not define themselves by marriage or a male partner. Such comments by your own family members can silence your voice and deny you your own choices.'

'You are right. I remember feeling for the first time a kind of physical pain because my own uncle called me the ugly word, "lefetwa". He said I'm cold to men and will never marry.'

'That's so cruel.'

'The reality is that I could feel myself slipping further and further

47

away from my family, experiencing a kind of estrangement I had never thought would be possible. Visiting home, I would be present physically, answering questions and doing what was expected of me, yet my mind was elsewhere.'

'Understandably.' You chewed for a few moments more. 'I broke with most of my family when I took a woman as a lover for the first time after my divorce.'

Your directness shocked me. I don't know if you could see it on my face. 'Have you had many women as lovers?' I surprised myself with my own direct approach.

'Four relationships. The others were just flings. And you?'

I shook my head, embarrassed. But there were crushes – like the one I had on you.

Gina, I think you and I talked until midnight that night. You didn't go back to your hotel. You caressed my neck, my face and my hair as we lay on my bed. Your teeth glittered like polished pearls.

That was the first night we spent together. Do you remember, Gina?

You started to stay over at my house more frequently. And gradually I told you more about my relationship with my family. We were lying in a bubble bath together one evening, my back against your breasts, when I told you how my mother once asked me to come and visit my grandmother's grave. 'She was with my uncle, whom I loathed. My uncle said I was bewitched because I didn't have a husband. My mother always believed everything my uncle said. We went to Brits, and the whole family enjoyed their traditional beer. They then tried to exorcise me. They did some traditional rituals for me and slaughtered a goat so that I could find a man. My mother told me that she was worried that I would be a woman in middle age who has never settled with her own family. Imagine, I was only thirty years old then.'

'Did they not respect that you had been building your career as a doctor?' Your lips were close to my ear.

I shook my head. 'Completing six years of studies and two years of practical to call myself a doctor was nothing in their eyes compared to finding a husband.'

'That is ridiculous.'

'During the rituals they performed for me, my mother prayed to the ancestors until tears streamed from her eyes. It disturbed and humiliated me.'

'I know what it's like to appear normal but to feel yourself swaying,' you commented. 'You can tell me everything.'

You were such a good listener. I relaxed against your body, the warm water of the bath soothing me. More incidents spilled from my memory and spewed from my mouth. 'One day my mother told me that my cousin was getting divorced. She tried to convince me that it was not a sin in our Setswana culture for me to marry him. I mean, what bullshit is that?'

'What? This is sick. I hate it when fellow women participate in patriarchal nonsense that oppresses their own.'

'That's exactly what I told her. Imagine, she said she would like to talk to my uncle to arrange my marriage to his son. Actually, it was a cultural thing, she said. Then, three days later, my sister called me to say my mother was admitted to the hospital. But something happened there at the hospital that irritated me.'

'What happened?'

'When I went to see her, my mother told me that seeing her first-born daughter married and pregnant would make her recover from her sickness. In other words, she was sick because of me. I could not take it any longer.'

Gina, as you can tell now, I remember those nights we shared together very well. Those four months that I stayed with you was the only interlude in my life in which I approached a state of contentment, containment, and perhaps happiness. The rain, the hot Joburg nights, the stories we shared about memories of our past and the hopes of our future, erased all the pain in me. Some nights when you lay in our bed asleep, I would pour a glass of wine and carry it to the balcony. There I would delve into your books that I had read so many times before. Bit by bit, after my long months of silence and solitude, I began to feel like I was no longer alone.

One night, after we had made love, I put my head on my pillow, my eyes open, filled with tears. I just could not believe that I was about to make a big confession to you.

'I killed her.' The words came automatically.

'What?'

'I killed my mother.'

You stared at me as I continued. 'I put an overdose of morphine in her veins. When she was in the hospital, I went there with a syringe full of morphine concealed in my purse. It's easy to get when you're a doctor. I added it to her IV while she was sleeping. She died peacefully. The hospital never said anything about it. They must have suspected a mistake on their part and would never admit to that. I paid for the funeral. But this thing has been eating me inside for the past year. I never had peace after that.'

I was surprised you did not look shocked or as if you judged me. If you were in shock, you hid it well. I felt your warm arm slide around my waist. Now that I am re-evaluating our time together I can only guess what you really thought when you heard those things.

'I understand,' you said. 'Your act, although I can't condone it, was a way of protecting yourself from her words and actions that demeaned you.'

'I was just tired of her asking me when I am having her grand-children all the time. As if she didn't know that I had once had to have an abortion. Each time we spoke, she would ask me that horrible question. I did not want a man forced on me. With her alive, I would never have been free of that.'

'I don't know if I would have acted the same. But I do understand where you're coming from.'

Your hands removed the ache from my body, heart and mind. You reminded me of the pleasure of being caressed and cuddled.

I tried to tell you more, but I could only sob. You then raked my back in circles with your fingernails.

'It's okay.'

'After her funeral, my uncle also asked me the same question. He wanted to know when I would get married. As a single black woman, I was just a problem to everyone, he said.'

'Oh no. Him too?' you asked, holding your hand high, your fingers spread as if you wanted me to stop talking. But I knew you were listening.

'Yes. I felt a suppressed fury rise like bile up my windpipe when he said that. Right then, I wished I could open my veins and drain my family blood from my body. I knew he had to go, too. I had felt his misogyny since I was a child. His death was a very simple thing to plan. It was during the unveiling of my mother's tombstone that I put poison in his beloved Jameson whiskey. He had a heart attack and died hours later after vomiting blood.'

'I guess that was the only way at that time you felt you could be free.'

'I just felt tired of the humiliation I was undergoing at home. This was the time in my life that I fell on *Men for Hire* and your other books as the only door out of my emotional turmoil.'

'I don't judge you. As African women, we have no youth and no freedom in this world. The moment our breasts develop our families immediately expect us to be someone else's wife or mother.'

'It is your books that helped me not to be lonely or scared.'

'I'm glad that, despite your family's exhortations, you resolutely refused to get married,' you said. 'The male energy can be both physically and psychologically violent. They colonise you and plunder you, and then blame you if you struggle with instability.'

Our domestic bliss continued. I went to work at the hospital and you stayed in our house to write. I was floating with the feeling that you accepted me completely. That there were no secrets between us. Do you recall that one conversation we had about our relationship, Gina? You said: 'I feel that my previous lover desired me from a position of weakness, and not adoration. With you, I feel at home because home is a person and not a place.'

'I feel the same about you. It is hard to find a person to love without blame or boundaries,' I remember whispering in your ear. 'I have never felt better physically, mentally and spiritually than I feel right now.'

A day before you left, everything changed. We lay in bed in the morning. You turned your head slowly towards me and cupped my cheeks in your soft hands.

'All my life I have tried to avoid permanent intimacy,' you said. 'I think I have to go.'

'What do you mean? Go where?' I asked, bewildered. But deep down I already knew that you were abandoning me.

'I need to go my own way, Sanaa.'

'Why?' I was shocked. 'I thought we had a special bond.'

'Nothing personal. It is just that if I sleep with someone for more than a few months, I usually become increasingly in need of my own space. I'm a writer, remember? That's why you don't see a ring on my finger.' You sighed. 'Four of my previous lovers continue to harass me on Facebook and call me names because of this. I hope you will not do the same.'

I did not understand how, just like that, despite my pleading, you could leave the following day. From the day you left, I couldn't sleep, was tortured by headaches, and almost unable even to go to work. I had to shut down that part of my brain that made me see you even when you were no longer there. I would wake up in the middle of the night, unable to go back to sleep. I felt exhausted. All I could do to calm myself was to read your work or walk around my neighbourhood. I ate all the food in the fridge. When

I stayed in bed, each time I closed my eyes, I would have the feeling that I was drowning. During the night, I would go over to the window and look into the darkness like someone leaning out over the abyss. Sometimes I would ask myself if you really existed, or if it was all just an illusion ...

And then, one day, I saw your new book in a shop window on the way home from the hospital. I stopped, and went in and bought it. I knew I was probably just torturing myself, trying to connect with you again. I read your now bestselling novel straight through the night and was speechless.

But now, at last, I am writing to you, Gina. Because I want you to know that I know. I know what you did. I know how you used me. I know your hypocrisy. And the irony is that you're the only one I can say this to. After all, how can I ever claim that story as my own without implicating myself? Were your previous lovers 'harassing' you for the same reason? What can I do now but congratulate you on your new bestselling novel with that taunting title, *My Lover's Secret*.

DISPLACED

The sky looked dirty the evening that Madoda Boya came home from his piece job to find his Rey Street home flattened. The street was cordoned off from one end to the other with police on foot and in vans patrolling. From a distance, it was already clear that piles of rubble were all that was left of the houses that once lined the street. His house had been reduced to one of these piles. Simile, his wife, and their two children, Nathi and Xolani, were nowhere to be found.

Madoda had left before sunrise that morning to go work in Baas Viljoen's garden in Benoni. It was just after six p.m. now and he had his day's pay in his pocket. He was carrying a plastic bag that contained food and clothes. But somehow the whole landscape of Kofifi had changed in his absence. It was not just his home at Rey that was gone. Toby Street, Gerty, Morris and many others were also destroyed. It was as if some natural disaster like an earthquake had happened, but the presence of police vans and bulldozers suggested otherwise.

The faces of his twins and wife sprang clear to Madoda's mind. He was quivering convulsively. At the corner of Rey and Edward Streets, a policeman wouldn't let him pass the barricade. The street was littered with different kinds of objects. There was a blackened saucepan without a handle on the left, a broken chair on the right. One left shoe, bottles, coal baskets and other broken items were scattered across the road.

'What do you want here? Can't you read the sign?' shouted the police officer. 'You are not allowed to enter here.'

'Please, my baas. I live there. I . . . I used to live there. What happened? Where are my wife and children?'

'Where were you when we told people to get ready to be moved? You thought it was a joke?'

The rumour about the imminent forced removals had been lingering for about a month or two in the township. Their beloved Kofifi was to become an area for whites only. But how is it possible that it happened today, on 9 February? Hadn't the government set the date as 12 February? In any case, the community had been adamant that they would not budge. There had been several meetings by the community leaders, banners, graffiti on people's walls, pamphlets, handouts, placards on the roads and so forth, saying: *Don't get in the lorry. We're not moving. Resist apartheid.* No one imagined the proposed removals to be a serious threat since large numbers were protesting and marching against it. The last march happened only two days ago. Many of the residents refused to fill in the forms the government sent for the allocation of new houses in the place they wanted to ship them off to. Madoda was one of those who had resisted. But now, here, before his own eyes were the flattened homes, his family and neighbours vanished.

'Do you know where my family was moved to, baas?'

'How the fuck should I know? I don't keep track of every black bitch and her brats. They've been allocated somewhere.'

None of Madoda's neighbours or friends had known exactly

where the new place was that the government wanted them to relocate to. Rumour was that the location was somewhere further away from the city and beyond the mine dumps. Some claimed it was to the west of the city. Others pointed to the south where there was a huge cattle farm. Where would he begin to look for his family?

'Please, baas,' Madoda said, appealing to the policeman again. 'I just want to check under that stone at the remnants of the gate if there is a message from my wife and kids. I used to live there, and my wife used to leave a message and keys to the house under that stone.'

'I said go back, boy. Are you deaf?'

Madoda's shoulders slumped, his finger twirling a loose thread on the hem of his shirt. As he pleaded again, his voice cracked.

'Please, baas, I was—'

'Do you want to die?'

The officer cocked his gun. Madoda looked at him in fear and bafflement. He then retreated, shaking his head, his arms dropping limply to his sides.

'No, baas. It's just that my wife always leaves the keys and messages there for me.' He again pointed at the huge stone next to what used to be a gate to his home. 'I was thinking maybe she left a message to say where they were being moved to.'

'You can't pass here or I will shoot you dead.'

Madoda gazed at the officer, searching his face with his eyes, trying to estimate the truth in what he was saying. 'Please, baas,' he began again.

'Just fuck off. Can't you see I'm busy here?'

The bulldozers were demolishing what used to be MaMshengu's shebeen nearby. This is where Madoda sometimes enjoyed his skokiaan brew and mbaqanga music on weekends. As he walked, he kept looking around apprehensively. Further demolitions were taking place at what used to be Mr Mini's coal yard. Mr Mini was one of the community leaders who had led the protest two days ago.

Madoda's courage began to wane when he thought of the way he had been dismissed by the policeman. Picking up his pace, his eyes searched for a face he could recognise among the few scattered people left in the streets. Most of them were as clueless as he was. Some had, like him, just come back from their workplace to find their families gone without a trace. He could hear the noise of his boots on the road that now looked like muddy gravel. Tears of anger, held back, pressed against his eye sockets. He had walked the same street that morning around four-thirty on his way to work. His wife and kids were still sleeping then. That was the last memory he had of them.

The grass turned gold on top of the nearby mine dumps as the sky slowly darkened. Bulldozers, loaders, graders and compactors were still busy at various locations. Ahead of him, a roof collapsed in a heap of dust and debris. As a result of the dust that lay everywhere on the street, and flew up at the merest movement, he himself was covered in dust. The night was rising up in waves, devouring the remaining buildings. He was afraid of walking in the dark ever since he had been robbed of his pay one night a year ago by the Berliners gangsters. In no time the sky turned a dark purple with sharp little stars. The police and the demolition workers were retiring for the night. Madoda's eyes were liquid with a hopeless will to understand what was happening. What was he to do? He shook his head. Tears streamed down his face. He was defeated.

He reached the ruins of a house near the main road with most of its walls still standing. A few people had lit a fire in what used to be a room of the house. He walked slowly towards them. Five men were standing round the fire warming themselves. Within him, he felt knife blades opening his body whenever he thought about his family and about his destroyed home. He was sniffling and wiping his eyes.

'Can we help you, my brother?' one of the men asked from beside the fire. The man looked a bit drunk. His eyelids were rounded over slightly protruding eyeballs. His nose was broad and grooved. Madoda recognised him as Mr Shange. The man's unshaven cheeks were covered in stubble, and his hair, some of which was long and some short, stood up on his head. To Madoda, it was as though Mr Shange had suddenly grown old and weary.

Mr Shange used to live in Morris Street, not far from Madoda's own home. They often met at MaMshengu's shebeen where they drank skokiaan and listened to mbaqanga and kwela music. Madoda heaved a sigh of relief to have found someone he knew.

'Mr Shange, so you also missed the removal trucks?'

'No. I was here in the morning. I almost soiled myself when they destroyed my home. I was scared.'

'What happened? You refused to climb on the truck?'

'It's a long story.' He licked his lips, wetting them in preparation for rigorous work, and Madoda knew Mr Shange was going to relay one of his drawn-out tales that he was known for. At MaMshengu's, men would gather round to listen to his stories, but Madoda feared that this tale was going to be a hard one to hear.

'About two thousand policemen, armed with handguns, rifles, dogs and knobkerries showed up at around seven this morning,' Mr Shange began, setting the scene. 'The police chief was walking about the streets and using a loudhailer to order people out of their houses. All of us – men, women and children – came out to see the police waiting for orders to demolish and level the houses we'd lived in for decades. Can you believe that? I have spent a lot of money to build our house. Imagine having your hard-earned property taken away in seconds by the bulldozers.'

When he spoke, Mr Shange tended to send a saliva shower on those close to him because of his two missing lower teeth. Madoda moved slightly away but continued listening. Mr Shange shook his head as he started speaking again. 'We were astounded and scared, gathering in the streets. The police chief said, *Listen to me carefully.* He told us we had only two hours to pack our belongings and put them on the pavement so that the trucks could come and collect us and our possessions to transport everything to the new place. *This is an order. Failing to do so is a punishable crime*, he said. He threatened that we would either be arrested or buried alive inside our houses by the bulldozers if we did not comply. The message was repeated over and over in Afrikaans, English, isiZulu and Sesotho, to make sure we heard and understood.'

'What did you do?' Madoda asked.

'What could we do? We were dazed and distressed in the streets, crowding together. Some crossed and linked arms, in solidarity.

That gave some short-lived comfort. There was widespread panic when the first lorries drove at speed past the shops near Victoria Street. They threw up dust as they stopped at the corner. Elsewhere, the hooves of the police horses broke the dirt crust as they beat the ground and it formed dust clouds around them. The streets swelled with people minute by minute. Women, men, children stood there bewildered while some cried openly. Everyone was looking for someone to hug or say goodbye to.'

Mr Shange shivered even though he stood close to the fire. All the men around him were silent, listening to the narration with grave faces.

'But there were some of us who resisted, who wanted to fight back. At the corner of Edward and Rey Streets, a few young men and women gathered in nervous groups. They were shouting at the police with indignation. I saw Mr Mini standing on a makeshift podium of a steel bath, making what sounded like a political speech.'

Madoda remembered walking past Mr Mini's flattened coal yard that evening. Mr Mini used to sell coal and firewood, as well as bread and milk at the shop that was demolished. Recently, Mr Mini had taken on the role of land activist, community leader and a messiah for the people of Kofifi.

Mr Shange quoted Mr Mini's words from that morning: '*They took everything from us, our homes, our dignity, our families, our land, our women … They are now wiping out from the history of this place all traces of our cultural presence as black people. They are determined to destroy all our traditions and our whole memory.* He was encouraging us: *Black man, you're on your own. Please wake up before it is too late. Resist the removals.*'

Spit flew from Mr Shange's lips as his tale picked up pace: 'Minutes later, the police had circled the makeshift podium with their dogs. The breathing of the leashed dogs came faster, with panting lungs, even though they were standing still.

'But Mr Mini wasn't done. *We must fight back, comrades*, he said. *Sofasonke maqabane. We must pledge to die together.* He told us that Comrade Jali has been writing letters to the city council authorities. And they have scouted the place the government is sending us to. *For those of you who are not aware*, he said, *it is a place far worse than this. It is a place full of grass and snakes because it used to be a farm.* Mini indicated that the new place is far away from the city beyond the distant mine dumps. *There is a shortage of housing, electricity and water in that goddamn place*, Mr Mini said. *We want the city to build more houses for our people here, and not there.* Then he shouted, *Amandla! Power. Black power!*, and we all replied, *Awethu!*, raising a fist in the air.

'What he said next, I will never forget.' Mr Shange paused for effect, looking at each of the men around the fire in turn. 'The truth of it is engrained in my memory. Mr Mini said: *Kofifi has been our home for many years. We are aware that as black people we have been conditioned for generations to appreciate the value of adaptability. But we cannot keep on adapting to segregation and poverty that is engineered by apartheid forces. Every kind of apartheid power is a form of violence against our people. We must continue to fight, for us and for our future generations. We must never give up.* And listen carefully to his last words: *There will come a time when neither the power of the apartheid forces nor any kind of segregation will exist if we fight this war together.*'

The men around the fire nodded in agreement.

'What did the police do?' Madoda asked, fearing the worst for poor Mr Mini after such an inciting speech in front of the apartheid forces.

'Well, of course, the chief police officer got angry hearing Mr Mini speak. He fired three shots into the air. There was a bit of a commotion that settled after a few minutes. The crowd and Mr Mini on the podium went quiet. The police chief shouted for Mr Mini not to try to be smart with them. *You will regret it because you will be shot dead*, the officer said with such rage-filled eyes flickering this way, then that.

'Then that police officer began walking towards the small group of people who had gathered along the pavement. I was standing among this group. I'll never forget that ugly-looking bastard. His long nose stuck sturdily from the middle of his bloated face. The sun had turned it orange like a carrot. He pointed at our group and said that if any of us tried to be clever with the government, we would be jailed or shot dead. *Do you hear me?* he asked. *Do you think this is a joke?*

'But Mr Mini was defiant. *Ons dak nie, ons phola hier. To hell with apartheid and its spies*, he said bravely from the podium. His voice took on a bitter, stubborn tone. He said the police could go tell their apartheid government that we were not going anywhere.

'The furious police chief commanded: *Take this piece of shit to jail now. If he tries to resist, shoot him in the head*. He told his men to take *anyone who tries to be a hero* in the van too.

'Without offering any kind of resistance, Mini folded his hands behind his head and arched his body like a bow. It was like something he had been waiting for all along, or at least something he was used to. He allowed himself to be handcuffed by two police officers. They then dragged him to the parked yellow van on the side of the road.'

'You are lucky that you were not arrested as well,' Madoda said.

Mr Shange clenched his teeth as if in pain. 'Luck had nothing to do with it. I almost *was* arrested. They set the dogs on the group of us who were standing there, supporting Mr Mini. We ran away.' He paused and touched his calf. Now Madoda saw the leg of his trousers was torn and there was a bloody wound in his flesh. 'This is what one of the dogs did to me. I pretended to be dead when the policeman commanded the dog to let me go. Otherwise, I would have been rounded up and jailed like a few others.'

Mr Shange's voice had a peculiar sound, which made Madoda feel sorry for him. Because of the painful wound on his calf, Mr Shange sat down on a large piece of rubble with some effort. He brought his hand up and wiped from his lip a last bit of dribble that his tongue could not reach.

All this time, Madoda had been feeling both impatient to ask Mr Shange if he knew anything about his wife and the twins, and at the same time afraid to do so – afraid that Mr Shange would tell him something horrible. Having them moved to some un-known location was bad enough, but if they'd been caught in conflict with the police . . . He cleared his throat and braved the question: 'I was not aware Mr Mini was arrested. I came back this evening to find my family gone and our house flattened. I have no idea where my wife and kids are. Do you perhaps know where the people were taken to? Mr Mini seemed to know the location.'

'My brother, most of us here have also lost members of our families. But tomorrow we are going on a mission to search for this new place. You can join us if you want. We will start walking at dawn. We heard they have been taken to a location south-west of the city beyond the mine dumps.'

'Well, I tried to get some information from a policeman and he nearly shot at me.'

'You asked the white police about your wife and children?' said one of the people around the fire mockingly. 'Did you expect him to identify your wife?'

'Not really. I assumed that maybe, since he was responsible for relocating and demolishing our street, he had a map or photos of the new place or something. I was hoping he had a list of the people and the places where the trucks may have taken them.'

'My brother, I think you were expecting a lot from those bastards. Those people have not one drop of human kindness. Anyone who has ever struggled under apartheid brutality knows how extremely expensive it is to be black in this country.'

All the men around the fire nodded. Madoda concentrated on the one who scratched his rough beard with dirty nails before he spoke. He remembered him as the feared Big John of the Spoilers gang. He was standing opposite Mr Shange, and Madoda could see his hollow cheeks and the pale chapped lips. He had heard that Big John was released from jail a week ago after serving twelve years for beating a man to within an inch of his life at Back of the Moon, which was at the corner of Gibson and Milner. The man was now so thin that there were folds at the back of his trousers.

'I think you were expecting a miracle from the white police officer,' Big John said as he rubbed his hands in front of the fire. 'For white people, blacks are like antelopes. Our faces all look the same. I saw it when I was in jail. Expecting a white police officer to know a black person by name is like looking for a black goat on a moonless night. Don't you know that these white people can identify five hundred breeds of dogs but will mix up their black workers? I, Big John, will take you to the new place in the morning.'

'I guess you are right,' said Madoda. 'But I had to give it a try.'

'There is infinite hope, but not for us,' said Mr Shange as he put his hand on Madoda's shoulder. 'Yet God is great. You will be expected to pay one rand to Big John to lead us to the new township, the apartheid government's promised land. Big John is our Moses.'

The evening was lost to the barking of the abandoned dogs, owls in the trees, and the sound of police sirens. Clouds covered the face of the moon. Madoda shared the food he was carrying with all five men around the fire. Then he tried to get comfortable on the hard ground for the night. But he could not sleep. Each time he tried to catch a nap, he saw shadows pass by the abandoned walls of this ruin, which caused him to lose all orientation.

His brain was picturing his wife and two children. What happened that day was like waking up from sleep with a heaviness caused by unremembered dreams. He pictured the new settlement as a jungle in which he would spend the rest of his life. He felt there would be violent and troubled days ahead. His ears were filled with a penetrating hissing that seemed to overpower all his senses.

'Get some sleep. We have a long walk to do tomorrow,' Mr Shange said from where he sat next to the dying embers of the fire as he saw Madoda was still awake.

'It will be especially long because of that bad leg you have,' Madoda pointed out.

'Don't worry about me. I will manage.'

A little before dawn, the cold became severe. Silence seeped into them along with the cold. The wood ran out and the last flames died down. Without success, Madoda tried to revive the dead fire with his shaking hands. The darkness was thick, almost solid in the absence of light.

At the break of dawn, they met up with other men, women and children who had been separated from their family members during the removals and who had also spent the night in uncertainty. They walked in groups to the new settlement beyond the mine dumps. Madoda and Mr Shange were in the third group that was led by Big John. Their shoes crunched on the gravel path. Flat rays of the promising sunrise were beginning to fill the treetops and the mine dumps ahead. Mr Shange walked with a limp, his whole body tilting to the right every time he planted that injured foot on the ground. The other leg kicked plumes of dust just to stay in balance as he walked on. His face looked consumed by the anxiety of the present moment. At regular intervals, they had to hurry to catch up with Big John and others, and Mr Shange had to trot awkwardly in order to stay alongside Madoda.

'Kofifi – I will remember that place. I wonder what the new place will be like,' reminisced Mr Shange. 'I will miss going to Undermoon Hall to listen to African jazz.'

'That is depressing,' Madoda said. 'But at the moment my concern is whether I will be able to locate where my wife and kids are.'

The morning was starting to set fire to the eastern sky. A weary sun was climbing slowly up to usher in yet another day over an ungrateful earth. The wind blew softly in the trees by a little stream. A tired-looking Mr Shange was now lagging behind as if he were going to face castration. He stopped at the little stream to soothe his leg in the water, but hurriedly withdrew it, because the touch caused him to shudder involuntarily.

'If it were not for the forced removals, I would be going to the jazz session at the Undermoon tonight.'

'Perhaps we need to forget about Kofifi in order to focus on what lies ahead,' said Madoda as he bent low to clear the drooping branches of a tree.

'Now you sound like those people who were happy when they heard about the relocation because they believed the promises of homes with proper toilets and water. Did you notice that it was mostly only the lodgers who were happy? That lot were all too pleased to cooperate with the authorities when they came to warn us about the move.'

Madoda had heard that some of the lodgers even bad-mouthed their landlords and spied on the gangs in Kofifi, such as the Russians, the Americans, the Gestapo and the Cowboys, all in the hopes that this would please the authorities who would then give them their own homes. He didn't like being compared to them and opened his mouth to speak.

But Mr Shange continued: 'How can I forget that special place? Forgetting is like dying, my brother. It is the same as surrender.'

Madoda quickly interrupted before the old man could say anything more. 'What I mean is that we must now channel our thinking to the future in this unknown new jungle they have dumped us in. Kofifi has ceased to exist.'

'The future is also in the past, my brother, and the past is in the present. But I do worry about the future. I'm not sure whether my wife will take me back after our fight this previous Sunday,' said Mr Shange. 'I'm not even sure she is still alive.'

'What happened?'

'Well, she confronted me after she found out about my affair with Sive. That lady who used to work at the Undermoon box office. I fought with my wife because of her.'

'Sometimes our mistakes correct us.'

The two walked in silence for a while. Madoda's memories were as shattered as those houses they'd left back in Kofifi. The sun was rising, causing a dazed city to appear behind them. The trip seemed to know no destination. Madoda could feel the sweat running down his arms, between his nipples and at the back of his knees. But in his mind's eye, Madoda could see his wife and children running towards him and showing him his new home, their faces beaming.

Mr Shange was limping behind Madoda. He could hardly keep to his feet. A bird beat its wings and flew off, lost in the brightly lit sky.

They walked for about five hours, slowed by Mr Shange's limp. Madoda felt his boot soles sinking into deep sand. He was inconvenienced by the mass of fine sand that filled his boots near the mine dump. The sand was warm on the surface and cold underneath. His forehead was pouring with sweat.

Just after the mine dump, they could see the structures of identical matchbox houses below. Ahead of them, a twisting wind lifted the dust on the path. The sky suddenly looked lower. Its brightness was dizzying, preventing Madoda from seeing clearly.

As they drew nearer to the new township, he was surprised to see children playing in the fields surrounded by the tall grass. He wondered at the resilience of children and knew adults would find it much harder to adapt.

There were several tall blue gum trees lined up along the dusty road. A huge black bird sat on top of one of the branches. The bird didn't fly away when it saw the new people coming into the township. It stayed on the tree, but eventually took to the air and circled and circled as if fascinated by the matchbox houses below and the enormous responsibility of having to fend for itself in the new township. Madoda looked at the bird and then at the straight strong trunk of the blue gum tree. Its roots that were struck down into the ground, the green branches hanging loosely over its top all made him experience a feeling of uncertainty. He felt like a time traveller who had voyaged into an unknown society.

'I wonder if they have already named this place. It would be interesting to see what name people come up with,' Madoda said.

'All I know is that Big John says there is not even a cinema in this new jungle.'

'So, its name is Jungle? What a name!'

'No, I call it a jungle. But I've heard Big John call it "Ndofaya, k'suka maphepha". I guess people will retain the old names of where they come from, like Kofifi, Western, George Goch, and the rest,' said Mr Shange.

On their entrance into the new township, Madoda and Mr Shange saw small uniform houses surrounded by tall grass. Their group had now spread out. Madoda remained with Mr Shange while the rest went off in twos and threes. Big John had gone back to Kofifi to get more people to walk with to the new township. This was his new way of making money.

Seeing the smoke that came from some of the chimneys made Madoda feel hunger gnawing at his stomach. Mr Shange's face looked tired, like a child's needing to sleep after staying up late. Madoda gave him a slap on the back which made him stagger a bit. From the side of the road, people watched them, or that's what Madoda thought, although perhaps they didn't even notice them. The smell of meat drifted across from one of the houses, titillating Madoda's nostrils.

Ahead of them, a road opened out. 'These houses all look the same,' said Mr Shange, his shoes squelching as he trod in the grey mass of mud. 'Have you noticed that there are similar fruit trees planted in every yard?'

'Yes, I've noticed peach trees, apricot trees and plum trees inside the tiny yards of the few houses we have passed so far. Look at the long grass along the street and in some of the yards. Mr Mini could be right – there are probably snakes here.'

Mr Shange reeled forwards, his body shaking all over, and he could hardly stand on his feet. He stopped, took out a handkerchief and blew his nose.

'How are you feeling?' said Madoda.

'The pain in my calf is terrible,' Mr Shange said, the corners of his mouth drooping. 'But I'll survive.'

A boy walked past them, hands on his hips, his shoes kicking up little puffs of dust. The sun was now very hot. The few clouds above did not give much protection.

'Where do we even start?' asked Madoda. 'Do you think we should enter house by house and ask people if they have seen our families? Or should we just walk on with the hope of meeting our families on the street?'

'That is not possible,' Mr Shange said. 'I'm already tired and my leg is swollen, as you can see. I can't walk any more.'

'Maybe we must just ask the people where the council offices are, or maybe a church could also help us.'

'Big John mentioned that there is a superintendent who has the people's register and allocated houses.'

At this point, Mr Shange limped slowly and badly along the uneven dusty street. He was trying to put only the outer edge of his limping foot on the ground. Hobbling irregularly alongside Madoda, he tried hard not to put his weight on his injured leg. His eyes were a bit wild, almost frantic.

Seeing that Mr Shange could now barely walk, Madoda decided they should go to a house where they saw both windows and the door open. A dirty lace curtain billowed out in the slight wind. A woman peeped through the window and then came rushing to the door. As they approached, Madoda thought the older lady had read his mind because at that moment she smiled tenderly at him. Her hollow eyes and dry lips seemed to belie the smile she was putting on. She had bulging cheeks as if she had hidden eggs inside them. Mr Shange took his hat off his head before he limped half a dozen steps inside the house.

The lady greeted them as soon as they sat on the wooden bench that was placed against the wall. There was nothing else inside that room. No plastering on the walls, no ceiling, no furniture. The woman, who looked to be around Mr Shange's age, introduced herself as MaSelepe. The place was dim, and the acrid smell of rot that Madoda had always disliked permeated the walls. Maybe it was Mr Shange's leg or a dead rat, he thought. The sitting room was very warm with the coal stove burning. By the doorframe, a gecko was chasing an insect. Interest flickered in the woman's eyes for a minute, then died.

'When I saw you coming, I was happy that my son was now back from jail,' she said. She must have been disappointed to realise they were not the visitors she had been expecting, Madoda thought.

'I'm Madoda Boya, and this is Mr Shange. Our families were among those removed from Sophiatown yesterday. We only just arrived. We've lost them and we are looking for our families.'

'I know. Yesterday, no fewer than six distraught people also asked me where they could find their families. It was chaos in the streets. Trucks continually arriving with more people. I sent everyone who asked to the town hall.'

'Where is the town hall from here?'

'It's a bit far – about forty minutes' walk that way.'

Madoda searched his pocket for a photograph and showed it to the woman. She studied it respectfully, then handed it back.

'No, I have not seen her. If I see or hear something, I will let you know. Just leave your address and contact details with me. I had a woman and her child yesterday looking for her husband, too. It is really sad what these white people are doing to us.'

At that moment, Mr Shange tried to straighten his swollen leg, perhaps to let the woman see it. The swelling had disfigured it. He then lowered his head, as though it helped him fight his pain. The woman saw, and was immediately touched by his terrible predicament.

'That looks really bad. Let me prepare water for you,' she said. 'You have to clean your wound for it to heal.'

'I know. It's just that I have been on the road since dawn.'

The woman looked away and then tried to change the topic. 'And do you also have a photo of your wife and kids?'

'I actually don't have one,' he replied and smiled almost shyly.

She put out her hand, like a mother does to stroke the face of a child, and planted her tender kiss on his forehead.

'Don't worry. You will find your family. God will guide you,' she said, nodding encouragingly at him. 'Just keep on searching.'

'Thank you for reviving my hope. I guess your words have already saved many for whom all hope seemed lost because of the disappearances of their loved ones.'

'It's in my nature to help. What I heard is that in this new township they have divided us according to our ethnicity. This part is for the Tswana and Sotho people. For the Zulus and Xhosas, you must start searching from the end.'

The woman went to the kitchen, and five minutes later she came back with a bowl of water that had been on the stove. She wet a washcloth. Holding it above Mr Shange's calf, she squeezed the water onto him, looking up as he murmured.

'Sorry, there is salt in the water and it will sting a bit, but it will help with the healing.'

Mr Shange grimaced. 'It is as if the salt water is nibbling at my flesh,' he said. 'But thank you, I know it is necessary.'

The salt water washed away the scab, penetrated his innermost flesh, allowing his blood to flow. Mr Shange breathed deeply, sighed, frowned and blinked frequently as if that was the only way to stand the pain.

'The superintendent must know where your families are. I hope you find them in good health.'

'It will be great to heal under the care of my wife and children.'

'I know love and pain have a symbiotic kind of relationship, just like a husband and wife. I lost my husband a few months ago. My son was arrested for planning a protest against coming to this crazy place, so now I am alone. I don't know when or if I will see him again.'

'I'm so sorry to hear that,' said Madoda.

'Everything passes, and time covers the world in rust. This too will pass.'

'We must not lose hope, even when they kill us and set dogs on us to bite us,' Mr Shange said.

'Death is a common thing to us black people under this apartheid regime, isn't it?' she said and looked up at the asbestos roof as if to cast her memory back a little. 'I can still hear my front door cracking and splintering under the assault by the police when they came to arrest my Thabo. Every day I live by hope that he will come back.'

The woman frowned and squinted, as though trying to help herself to remember. A good thought would not hurt to cheer her up, Madoda reckoned.

'He will eventually come back.'

'I hope so, my child. Although hope in this time of apartheid is too small.'

'But I'm sure it always forces itself through the eye of the needle. One day this apartheid will be a thing of the past. Our people will be free.'

'Maybe. But the past claws its way out. You can't bury it just like that. It's not like human flesh. And yet we need to move forwards. Now, let me prepare you some food and a room to rest before you continue with your journey.'

The woman disappeared into the kitchen. Madoda watched Mr Shange as he dried his leg. He then scooped up a small glob of Vaseline that the woman had given him with the tip of his finger before rubbing it around his wound. The remaining Vaseline on his finger, he smoothed onto his lips.

They both slept in exhaustion that night. The silence of the new township was amplified in the darkness. Madoda dreamt of hundreds of people being transported to the new township by trucks. His wife and twins were in one of the trucks. The soldiers did not allow him inside, as they claimed that it was full. Later, he would dream about his family arriving in the township. They were living underground, sunk deep in mud and darkness, feeding themselves on whatever the soldiers tossed into the sewerage pipes.

In the morning Madoda awakened from his heavy, almost comatose, sleep. A gecko, hanging directly above him, was studying him curiously. Madoda went outside where the sky was clearing. A ray of sunlight warmed his face. He brought his hands to his eyes, then rubbed. He had a bit of pain in his mouth, neck and chest, but other than that, he felt fairly rested and restored.

'Good morning, makhelwane,' a woman greeted him from next door.

'A beautiful morning to you, too,' he said.

She was hanging up some wet clothes on the washing line. The shadow cast by the clothes strung out along the line covered most of the yard and made it cooler. At the corner of the house, he saw two chickens scratching away.

'My name is Nokuthula. I live here.'

'I am Madoda. I came here yesterday trying to locate my family. I was not there when they moved my wife and children from Sophiatown.'

'All the luck with that. You must try the council offices. I know a few people found their families through it. Also, look at the wall once you are there. There are notices everywhere on the wall.'

'Thank you. I'm going there right away.'

Somehow the talk with Nokuthula made Madoda feel reborn with hope. That morning, he walked alone to the council offices where Nokuthula and MaSelepe had directed him. On his way along the dusty road, his hope faltered only once. What if she was dead? What if she resisted arrest and was shot? What if she was in jail? He shook his head violently to get rid of the idea. She was fine. He was going to find her.

Eventually, he reached a big building that was painted white. There was a long queue of people that was stretched around the building. While standing in the queue, he realised that this was the place where people got permits to live in the new township, registered for work placements, registered the birth and death of their loved ones, and so on. On the walls both in and outside the building were notices that were attached with chewing gum.

When it was his turn to be assisted, the officer told Madoda that he had no record of his wife and kids. Madoda even spent time checking the notices on the wall. There was nothing from them, although there were many other notices from people looking for family members, loved ones, old neighbours and friends. He decided to leave his own message on the wall:

> *My name is Madoda Boya. Right now I live in Ndofaya*
> *Zone 1. Please help me to locate my wife, Simile Boya,*
> *and my twin boys, Nathi and Xolani. We used to live*
> *at 36 Rey Street, Sophiatown-Kofifi. My twins are six*
> *years old. My wife is thirty-one years old. They disap-*
> *peared during the forced removals on Wednesday, 9 Feb-*
> *ruary 1955.*

He pinned the message on the wall with gum and left. When he came back to MaSelepe's that afternoon, he saw Nokuthula in her yard again.

'So, how did it go?' she asked.

'There was nothing, but I left a message.'

'It's good that you did that. One day God will answer your prayers.'

'I hope so. In the meantime, I also registered my name at the job recruitment officer. I will check with them again soon.'

'That's wonderful. I will keep praying for you.'

Madoda sighed. 'We lived life sweetly and bitterly in Kofifi. We were happy that we had a big yard for our twins to play in. Today, I don't even know where they are.'

'I know. Here we are not even allowed to walk at night. The police are always on the lookout. We are counted as if we are chickens. My friend's mother and father were slapped right in front of their children for not answering a policeman quickly enough. I hear that we can soon expect regular police raids of our homes. As if we haven't suffered enough.'

With neither of them having any luck in locating their families, Madoda and Mr Shange continued to stay at MaSelepe's house. She seemed happy to have the company. Neither of them had filled in the government forms for the allocation of houses when the government had first threatened to move them from Sophiatown, and according to the council offices, there were no houses allocated to them yet. Where their family members had found places to live was a mystery that refused to be solved.

On most days, Madoda walked the streets, hoping to glimpse his wife or boys. He showed her photograph to people without any luck. Trucks full of people kept arriving in this new township from other parts of Kofifi and further afield. They were all being thrown together here and needed to fend for themselves.

When they needed groceries, MaSelepe sent him on the long trek to the nearest shops. There were no stores in this new township yet, so he had to go very far. He used the opportunity to scout for his family, but he did not find them.

Returning to the house one afternoon, Madoda found MaSelepe in a happy mood. Mr Shange had taken a walk, his injury healing. She told Madoda that she had found a lead for him through a colleague at church. The house number he was given was within walking distance.

'My colleague says there is a woman with twins who lives opposite her house. Maybe you can go there and check tomorrow.'

'Thank you, MaSelepe. We can only live by hope in this complicated life.'

'Sometimes it is the very thing we cannot understand that makes life worthwhile.'

'We have suffered enough.'

'I know, my child,' she said as she stroked his cheeks and patted the back of his head with her cold, damp hand. 'But I trust this person who gave me this number. She is the elder at our church. She says her neighbour is a woman with your wife's description.'

That night in his bed, Madoda allowed himself some excitement and anticipation of being reunited with his wife the following day. He could hardly sleep.

So, it was with extreme disappointment that he arrived at the address MaSelepe gave him the next day to find a woman some years older than his wife.

Nights merged into days. February passed. March arrived, and the soil was beginning to crack with thirst. Madoda and Mr Shange had been roaming about the new township for more than a month now, going round and round looking for their families without success. The two of them visited the council hall without fail every day. With the passing of the days, Madoda's trousers looked as if they had originally belonged to someone bigger than him.

His friend, Mr Shange's wound had completely healed with the help of MaSelepe who washed it every day. They were still accommodated at MaSelepe's, but Madoda had started spending evenings at Nokuthula's house. She had told him that she did not like to cook for only one person and he should come over to eat with her. He found that she was easy to talk to and he went round there every night from then on.

'Strangely, I dreamt about my late husband last night,' she said one evening, touching and straightening the tablecloth in front of her. She had told Madoda before that her husband had died in the mines about a year and a half ago.

'Like they say, love is like God. It is everywhere, even in our dreams. Like God, love has millions of people in its image, but many people don't know it.'

'All I can tell you is that love and marriage is a gamble,' she said, avoiding his eye contact. 'Some people, like me, gambled unluckily with my husband and lost.'

Madoda sat there for a while without saying anything. He allowed Nokuthula's words to sink into his mind. Without warning, the memory of his wife and children came to him. As he sat there in Nokuthula's kitchen, his mind evoked alternately two images in which he now conceived of his wife and children. His mind told him that maybe she was dead, and that she had ceased to exist. She had become only a memory.

'I guess I also gambled unluckily,' he said to Nokuthula before he left.

In June, both Madoda and Mr Shange found work at a factory in Germiston through the recruitment office. A few weeks earlier, Mr Shange had managed to track down his wife when he finally spotted her on one of his many meanders across the township. But she was furious at him for getting into a fight with the police on the day of the removals and – in her words – abandoning her to travel to the new location on her own. In his long-winded account of their reunion to Madoda, he quoted her exact words, imitating the voice in which she had said them: '*And don't think that I've forgiven you for cheating with that slut from Undermoon.* Can you believe she spit those words in my face? And what's more, she said: *I've actually started to enjoy a life without you and now here you are, back again.* She said the family with whom she is staying has become like her own and she does not want to leave.' Mr Shange shook his head. 'What am I supposed to do? I'll let her be.' He looked seriously at Madoda and said, 'Perhaps some things are better left in the past.' Mr Shange kept staying with MaSelepe who was more than happy to have him in her home.

It was around this time that something changed in Madoda's friendship with Nokuthula. They were sitting on her couch one night reminiscing about good times in their former lives and with their respective spouses. As he talked about his wife, Nokuthula became quiet and tearful.

'Are you okay?' he said, putting a hand on her shoulder.

She touched his hand with both of hers, took it gently off her shoulder and held it in her lap. 'Dear Madoda, I am so sorry for the pain you are going through. I care so much for you. I would give anything for you to be happy. If I could bring your wife back to make you happy, I would. I just want to make you happy, Madoda.' She squeezed his hand tightly.

Madoda was overcome with emotion and with compassion for this beautiful woman who thought so highly of his well-being. Before he could think what he was doing, he leaned forwards and kissed her. She kissed him back, as if that were the one thing in the world she could do to make him truly happy.

Madoda and Nokuthula's friendship had by August developed into a strong love affair. He was now living with her in her house. He had closed the door on his wife and kids, not because he didn't love them any more, but simply because he felt that door didn't lead him anywhere. He had given up on the prospect of ever seeing them again. He had not seen his family for about six months now, but he still continued to meet up with his wife and children from time to time in his dreams.

With Nokuthula, he found some healing for the loss of his family. He found companionship and a cure for his loneliness. Nokuthula had allowed him to glide inside her heart with pride of ownership.

Then, one day, towards the end of August, a miracle happened. Madoda was with Nokuthula at the council office to register her sister who was visiting from KwaZulu. The laws required everyone visiting the new township to have a permit, otherwise they would be deported back to the rural areas. While Nokuthula was still busy registering her sister, Madoda went to the spot where he'd once attached his message. He hadn't checked it in a long while.

There, on the wall, sitting next to his message was one from his wife:

> *I hope this message finds you. This is your wife, Simile Boya. The kids and I have been looking for you. We live in a place called Dobsonville, house 855. I saw this message about three months ago. I went to the house you said you live in and found a woman called MaSelepe. She was sitting with a woman called Nokuthula. They both told me you left their place about a month ago and they didn't know where you had gone. I hope one day you will read this and come home.*

It was as if the universe, with its past, present and future, was gathered together into a single point before and after which nothing existed. Without looking back, he left Nokuthula at the council office and set off to get to Dobsonville by any means necessary.

JOHUSTLERBURG PRISON CELL

I was arrested for drinking and driving on a Friday night, just after Mandela Bridge. I was on my way home to Ridgeway, south of the city. It was not the first time it happened. Less than a year ago I'd been arrested on the same spot and taken to the Hillbrow Police Station. I don't know why I didn't learn my lesson. An intelligent person like me would have used a different road out of the city after having drunk the way I did. I guess that's what happens when you have a drink and a joint and party too hard at your usual hang-out spot. A joint always makes me forget important things like a police roadblock. I had spent all my money with my friends and forgot to leave some for what the Joburg police often call 'cold drink.'

What worried me most was not that I was driving my mother's car, but that I was a third-year law student at Wits University. As a law student, I should have known that having a criminal record would render my studies worthless. Rules are rules. I would never be allowed to practise, even if I graduated.

It was around eleven at night when about five of us were taken in a van to the Johannesburg Prison. Remember that lady called Ora, the actress from that soapie called *Johuslerburg Slay Queen*? She was there as well. In fact, I had seen her as they drove out of the parking lot at the Bannister Hotel. She had been drinking there with some guy – Jay Jay, as I later learned when I met him inside the cell. I felt pity for Ora. She'd pleaded with the female officer to let her off the hook.

'Please, I can't miss a call at five in the morning. I depend on this acting job for a living. I have a shoot tomorrow.'

'You should have thought about that when you were still drinking,' said the officer with a condescending smile. 'At least your producers will have a better storyline for your drama. You see, the breathalyser says you are way over the limit. Four point zero is a lot, sisi.'

A painful process of realisation began when our blood samples were taken at the police station. Ora cried hysterically. At first she resisted. She burst out into a crazy fit of rage, which I regarded as her acting character. Her dress lifted above her knees, exposing those shapely, bronzed legs. The two female officers overpowered and restrained her.

'If I were you, I would shut up and not cry now. You will need those tears, young lady,' the officer said to her. 'Since you like drama, you will be on the front page of the newspapers tomorrow morning.'

I started biting my nails. I always do this when I'm under stress. The taste of my misfortune stayed in my mouth.

When my father had bailed me out after my previous arrest, he had sworn that it was the last time. Now I had no choice but to call him again and beg for help. Knowing my father, I did so reluctantly.

'You have committed career suicide, boy,' my father said. 'I have been warning you about your abuse of alcohol and coming home late. We lent you that car so that you could attend classes, not go about drinking alcohol in nightclubs. Do you have any idea how much it cost me to make you a person? Give the damn phone to your officer so that I can speak to him.'

I could hear my mother speaking in the background but could not make out her words. My eyes came to rest on the male officer behind the charge desk. I switched the phone to loudspeaker and gave it to him.

'Officer, please lock that boy away for a week or more,' my father's voice sounded clearly. 'Even for ten years if you want.'

'But it's only for drinking and driving, sir.'

'I don't care, just lock him up. I don't want to see him for a while. Even when he is released, he must not come here. I will be there in the morning to fetch the car.'

My father hung up. I felt exhausted and stunned at the same time. The faces in the charge office looked at me with penetrating stares. I wiped my eyes with the back of my hand.

'You've heard your father,' the male police officer said, examining my face. 'But don't worry. Tomorrow you will be out.'

'Is there any possibility of being released now?'

'No, the detectives will only come in the morning to handle your cases. The matter is now between the detective and your arresting officer. We are only responsible for recording it on our computer system.'

'What do you suggest I do?'

'Mfanakithi, just admit your guilt to the magistrate court. You will be let out with a warning. The bail is one thousand five hundred rand, but you can only pay it tomorrow morning.'

With those words, I was thrown into a cell with other men. The air inside carried that harsh smell of prison life. I inhaled cigarette smoke and alcoholic ferments that came from about fourteen different mouths. The stench of urine and shit rose from the toilet in the corner. The odour clung to my skin like something sticky. On the dirty walls were lines of graffiti:

> *Martin from Malawi was here.*
> *Lindela is a shithole.*
> *Stop Afrophobia and Xenophobia. Africa must unite.*
> *Peace in Africa.*
> *Fees must fall.*
> *I suck a penis for free.*

In another corner of the cell were piles of folded grey blankets and thin blue sleeping sponges. A man stood and smoked a cigarette next to graffiti of what looked like an anus or pouted mouth being entered by an erect penis. By the door was a drawing of a rope around a neck. I started wondering if people entered the cell with flipchart markers. The graffiti that chilled me the most was scribbled near the small window. It said:

> *Ahmed Timol survived only four days.*

Terrifying pictures sprang to my mind and the walls curved over me. After my father, a former teacher and SACP member, had bailed me out last time, he'd given me the poem 'In Detention' by Chris van Wyk to read. It was about death in detention during apartheid and falling from the ninth floor. My father had also made me watch a documentary by Enver Samuel called *Someone to Blame: The Ahmed Timol Inquest.* I thought about this so graphically that it was as though I were floating in another time. *The birth of this country is steeped in blood*, I thought, some remembered phrase.

One of the inmates brought me back to the present. 'Welcome home, prisoner,' he said sarcastically. 'What do they call you?'

'Itu Masike.'

'Heita daar, Itu. I'm Jay Jay. Please lend me your cell, my outie. Mine has run out of battery and airtime. I need to call someone to organise bail money for tomorrow.'

Hesitating, I gave the man my cellphone. He looked harmless and very neat for a prisoner. After him, my phone went from one person to another until it also ran out of battery and airtime. At least I got to smoke their cigarettes in return.

'I heard the voice of a woman shouting,' said Jay Jay, looking as though through the walls at the charge office. 'What happened?'

'It was that actress Ora, being taken to a female cell. She resisted the drawing of her blood. She told them she was a Jehovah's Witness, but they would have none of that excuse.'

'Ora *is* a Jehovah's Witness,' Jay Jay said. 'I can't believe she was arrested. She was my passenger when I was arrested. I thought she took the car home after they arrested me. I have been trying to get hold of her, but her phone is off.'

'There was another roadblock less than a kilometre away.'

'Bastards!' Jay Jay clicked his tongue in disgust. 'Why focus on small matters of drinking and driving instead of solving big crimes like murder, drug trafficking and human trafficking? We only had a few shots of vodka.'

'What do you think will happen to us? You think they will release us?' someone asked the question I was also dying to ask.

'No, it has to go to court. I know how it works. I've been arrested for drinking and driving about six times,' said a man who was lying down on a sponge mattress. 'We are going home tomorrow. The law says we must be charged within twenty-four hours.'

'Yes, they are just waiting for us to sober up so that we can drive our cars. Maybe after three hours or so.'

'I work for the state. I can't afford to have a criminal record. Otherwise I run the risk of dismissal.'

'You need to bribe the police for your docket to go missing, my outie. After paying the bail, which is refundable, you must pay the arresting officer about two stina to make your docket disappear. That's how they work here.'

'But you can only have a criminal record once you're found guilty and sentenced.'

'You already have a criminal record because your fingerprints are in the system.'

'But I have not appeared in court yet to plead whether I'm guilty or not. How can I be a criminal?'

Then Jay Jay spoke again: 'But how could they arrest people for drinking? Some of us drink out of pure pleasure and not to kill anybody. There are those who drink because they cannot talk and they need to socialise – like that outie on the sponge playing with his phone. I drink to think better.' He shook his head. 'You see, I was arrested with Ora, who is my girlfriend. Now I'm forced to call my wife, to ask her to withdraw money from Ora's card to bail out both of us.'

'Usesmokweni, my outie. Why don't you ask someone instead of your wife? Give the police your card to withdraw the money?'

'I've tried, my outie. They say it's not allowed. Jail is a place of confession, rediscovery and plans. I just have to face the truth.'

Seconds, minutes and hours followed one another at a slow pace. A day seemed to have passed when in reality it had only been a few hours. It was after one in the morning and most inmates were sleeping. Only one or two people were still awake. Three new drunk inmates had just arrived. I was suffering from a bitter regret at having forfeited the perfect and suitable future that my father had worked hard to create for me.

Dawn was like the previous night, full of uncertainties. The cell still emitted its smell like that of an old unpleasant memory. All of us were sober now. We sat with morose expressions on our faces while silence enveloped us.

There was a jingle of keys, and the cell door opened. A ridiculous surge of hope arose in me. Two loaves of bread and cold tea in a two-litre Coke bottle was brought in by a policeman. The quiet guy in the corner and I were the only ones who didn't eat anything.

The night before, I'd noticed the quiet guy who sat in the gloom in the far corner with his head lowered. Most of the time he'd pretended to be playing a game on his cellphone, listening in silence. Sometimes he smiled mysteriously and moved his lips like someone talking to himself.

Thirty minutes later, an officer came to our cell again.

'Everyone with bail money, follow me,' he said. 'If you don't have the money, you will remain here until Monday when you go to court. Those of you who have the money will pay the clerk and will come back on Monday for your hearing.'

One after another, the inmates followed the officer. I was left alone with the quiet guy. A disturbing realisation dawned on me: There was no longer any question that my parents had given up on me.

'My outie,' I addressed the quiet guy, 'it seems like we are the only ones to spend the weekend here. What's your name? Mine is Itu.'

'I'm Andrew, but they call me Druza ko kasi.' He paused. 'Eish, Joe, I was hoping my friends would come back for me. I was coming from Maboneng ko Pata Pata when they arrested me. I was driving a friend's car. Ngisesmokweni.'

'My taima told me shit when I called him.'

'I wish I knew my taima. I would call him now. My mother keeps referring to him as an asshole when I ask.'

'Kuyafana, nje. Mine, it's like he doesn't exist.'

'I heard mine was my mother's school teacher somewhere ko kasi. Anyway, she had me at the age of seventeen when she was a learner.'

I reciprocated Druza's gesture of friendship by also being open about my relationship with my father. I told him about my father's incapacity for love and the fact that he did not show consideration for his children. We talked until around two in the afternoon, when an officer came to open the cell.

'Which one of you is Itu? You're wanted at the reception.'

I gave Druza my cellphone number and he said he would give me a call sometime. His eyelids flickered and his lips were pressed together when I left him. I followed the officer to the reception. There I was met with my mother's judgmental, inquisitorial gaze.

'Your father is very angry with you. He came here at around

eight in the morning to fetch the car. I thought he was coming to get you out, but then I realised that he didn't. That's why I came to fetch you. This is the very last time.'

Before we exited the prison gate, I thought about Druza. We had established a bond and I felt guilty about leaving him alone in the cell.

'Ma, can I please ask you for a favour before we go?'

'No. I said no more favours.'

'Please, Ma. There is a young guy in the cell. I'm afraid bad things could happen to him in the prison. He doesn't even eat. He is only twenty. Please can we bail him out?'

'Is he your friend?' I nodded. 'Okay then, as long as he will pay me back the money.'

'It is refundable,' I said.

Back inside the police station, an officer went to the cell to call Druza. Less than ten minutes later, we were back together again. Druza was biting his lower lip. He gave my mother his ID and she examined it quietly for a while. Then she paid his bail.

'Thank you, ma'am.'

'Itu will drive you to Soweto after dropping me off at home.' She turned to me, 'No more drinking.'

In the rear-view mirror of the car she scrutinised Druza's face where he sat in the back seat. Without a word, she played her favourite tune by Sona Jobarteh, 'Kaira.'

'So, your surname is More?' she asked.

'Yes, I'm using my mother's surname.'

'What's her name?'

'Dawn More.'

'And you were born in 1999, just a year after Itu,' she said almost to herself.

After that, my mother drove quietly to Ridgeway, as if she had forgotten how words were formed and uttered. We arrived at our house about thirteen minutes later. I invited Druza in for something to eat before I'd take him home. My father was watching a soccer game on TV. He ignored Druza but gave me a look of contempt.

To my mother, he said, 'So, you defied me and went to bail him out?'

'You should be happy that I brought your other son, too,' my mother said with a sharp edge to her voice.

'What do you mean?'

'Does the name Dawn More ring a bell? She was your student lover some twenty-two years ago? Why didn't you tell me that you had a son with her, huh? I only found out today by chance. His names are exactly as yours, Andrew Moeketsi More. Only the surnames are different. You can't tell me that you don't know about him.'

Druza and I stood there stunned. I looked at my humiliated father without warmth or feeling. I could sense a mixture of shame and resentment in him, his infidelity and hypocrisy exposed.

'I swear to God it's the first time I'm seeing him,' protested my father. 'Yes, I knew Dawn was pregnant. Then she ...'

My mother narrowed her eyes into slits. 'So you continued to have a baby with your Dawn?'

My father didn't answer. My mother kept repeating the name Dawn More again and again. It seemed to have scarred her, to be imprinted on her brain.

94

That was another family lesson for me: A wife never forgets the name of her husband's mistress. It will weigh on her chest forever like a heavy brick. It doesn't matter how long ago the affair was, or whether the other woman is still alive or dead. The sound of her name alone will trigger anger, hatred and hurt.

THE STALKER

He was following her every movement with his eyes. When she came out of the house, he was parked a little way down the street, in the borrowed car. She wouldn't see him, but he could watch her. He could see everything she did. She had a big handbag slung over her shoulder. It looked like it was bulging. What did she have in there? He would love to rummage through it. Perhaps he would get a chance later if he could get closer. He wanted to stay very, very close to her today.

She locked the house with those slender fingers of hers, put the keys in her huge handbag and started walking down the street. Her hips swayed in her black pants as she hurried along, the movement drawing his eyes to her round buttocks. Her braids swayed to the rhythm of her walk. She had taken care with her appearance.

He swallowed and started the car. Where could she be going? When she was far enough away, he started to drive slowly after her at an inconspicuous distance. He would find out her destination. He would follow her there.

It was a hot day, but the sky was threatening rain and thunder as he watched her get into a minibus taxi at Reverend S Modise Drive, Meadowlands, to Joburg city centre. She had a seat at the window and he could look at her profile before the taxi pulled away. Her lips were plump and she had put on lipstick that made them look wet. For a second, he thought she turned her head towards him, but she was staring blankly out the window. In the borrowed car, he followed the minibus taxi at a distance.

The sky was darkening overhead. He heard thunder and saw a few flashes of lightning.

In the city, the rain started to fall in large drops. Water gurgled loudly in the gutters and drainage. She got off at Bree Street, took out a black umbrella from her bag and unfurled it. Safe from the rain, she walked towards Braamfontein along Biccard Street. He parked the car at the side of the road and continued to follow her on foot. She was stylish in her tight black jeans and orange T-shirt. Men gave her melting looks along the road. He kept his eyes on her, missing nothing. With his gaze not once straying to his feet, his running shoes were submerged in a large puddle while trying to keep up with her. But he kept going, crossing at the traffic lights at Wolmarans Street. She would not get away from him.

She entered the ANEW Hotel Parktonian in Braamfontein. Her wet umbrella, which she had shaken a bit outside after closing it, was placed in an umbrella stand provided for guests inside the lobby. She looked around and her big white teeth were biting her shiny bottom lip slightly. Then a tall woman with short peroxided blonde hair approached her. The woman was wearing white shorts. Her calf muscles looked hard and the flesh of her thighs did not tremble. She flung her arms out wide as she walked towards the object of his surveillance and they greeted each other with a brief kiss.

Could this be a friend of hers? It was not one that he had ever seen before.

The two disappeared around a corner and he could no longer see them from outside. He entered the hotel lobby and walked in the same direction that they had. He reached the elevators but there was no sign of them. Numbers flashed at the top of the steel doors as the elevator climbed. It paused at the sixth, the eighth and the fifteenth floor before making its way down again. There was no knowing which floor she had disappeared to.

He went to the couch in the lobby from where he could keep an eye on the elevators. The day's newspapers were strewn on a coffee table and he picked one up to hold in front of his face as if he were reading. Everything had an air of cleanliness inside the hotel. He pretended to be one of the guests, or waiting for someone. No one paid him attention. In fact, the hotel was busier than usual that Friday.

After about twenty minutes, he saw the two appear again. She had changed into shorts with her orange T-shirt. The woman with the silvery blonde hair took her hand and they proceeded to the lunch buffet on the external wooden deck. The rain storm had ended as quickly as it had started. The air had cooled a bit, but it was still warm. They loaded food on their plates and took a seat at a table for two. She was just eating some salad, as if she were watching her figure. Her companion smiled at her over their plates. He watched as they ate and talked and laughed. At one point, she threw her head back as she laughed and he stared at her long, smooth neck.

When their plates were empty, they stood up and went to the reception desk. They were handed hotel swimming towels, which they threw over their shoulders. He did not rush to follow them when they approached the elevators again. This time he could assume they were headed to the swimming pool on the rooftop, dubbed the Skylevel. The hotel towels on their shoulders were a dead giveaway. He didn't want to be conspicuous by following them immediately.

Thirty minutes later he was at the Skylevel. The two of them were standing chest deep in the water. He bought a beer at the cocktail bar and took a seat at the far end of the counter. He'd brought the newspaper with him from downstairs and he alternated between pretending to read it and pretending to enjoy the panoramic view of the Joburg skyline. But what he was really doing was ogling the women in the swimming pool. When he glanced at them again, he caught them kissing – a deep passionate kiss. The object of his observations touched the ears of her lady friend tenderly. Their laughter echoed fresh and brilliant. An invisible aura of love was evident between them. At first he didn't believe it. He thought he was confused because of the beer he was drinking. Usually he was not that much of a drinker. Also, he could not see her face properly, as she was facing sideways. Her arms were hidden underwater. He could only see her bare shoulders.

Then he glimpsed her hands moving over her companion's chest as if feeling the woman's breasts. He felt validated but embarrassed. She tossed water over herself like a bird using its wings.

The women didn't seem to notice that there was a man who was watching them. They didn't seem to care if anyone saw them. Their laughter filled the bar.

He took out his cellphone and typed in the number he had memorised. At the corner of the swimming pool where their towels were, he heard her cellphone ring. They both ignored it and continued laughing and holding each other. He felt his chest bursting; he could not contain his outrage.

He stood up, and strode to the side of the swimming pool, closest to where they were bobbing in the water. His sudden appearance made their intimacy evaporate.

'Amahle, how long has this been going on?' He glared at her. 'You told me you had a job interview when you left home this morning. Is this what you mean by a job interview?'

Shock and terror reflected in her eyes. 'Ntando, what are you doing here? Did you follow me?'

'Hey!' the woman with the peroxided hair said. 'What are you, some kind of sicko stalker?'

'I'm her husband,' Ntando said through clenched teeth.

'Oh,' the woman seemed unfazed. 'You're *that* guy.' A contemptuous smile played around her mouth. Ntando turned away from her to his wife. 'Amahle, just answer me. Does your job interview involve kissing another girl in the pool?'

Amahle kept quiet. The other woman got out of the water and dried herself with a towel.

Quietly, Amahle followed her out of the swimming pool, and stood shivering and hopeless for a while before using her towel to dry herself.

'It's not what you think, Ntando,' Amahle said eventually. 'This is my friend, Samu.'

'Don't lie to me. I have been suspicious of you for some time now. Did you think I didn't see you answering late calls and WhatsApp messages? What about the couple of days you left me at home with our child, and told me you found a piece job in the city? Or all the times you told me you had a job interview and I had to take care of our son. Did you think I wouldn't suspect anything even when you only returned the next morning? You tried to distract me with the money and groceries you brought back, but I wondered whether you were having an affair. That is why I left our son with a friend today and borrowed their car so that I could follow you. I've been watching the two of you.'

'Just tell him the truth. He is a stalker,' Samu said as she finished drying herself. 'I'm tired of hiding our feelings for each other.'

Ntando felt he had nothing further to ask or confirm. He looked at Amahle for almost a minute without blinking. She met his gaze only briefly, then lifted both her hands to her face as if to smell them.

'Please, Ntando, I can explain.'

For a while, a rising anger clamped his mouth shut. He felt too weak to even speak to her. 'Explain what? That you are cheating on me with a woman? You're not even ashamed. I have paid half lobolo to your family thinking I was marrying a woman. I will have to demand my money back,' he said, his hands clasped at the back of his head. 'You're a slut, Amahle. A big whore.'

'Hey, don't call her that. You have no right to call my girlfriend that ugly name,' said Samu. 'Never.'

'What are you going to do? She is a slut. You're both sluts.'

'I will beat you up in front of everyone,' Samu threatened.

His eyes continued to bite into Samu. His fists were balled, ready for a physical fight, even if she was a woman. From the corner of his eye he saw the tall, thickset barman stepping closer to him and Samu, ready to jump in should they come to blows.

'This slut thinks she can take my fiancée and intimidate me,' he said, turning his head towards the barman.

There was a vicious *thwack* against the side of his mouth, an aching pain, and he fell into the swimming pool with a big splash.

'I warned you never to use that word again.' Samu was rubbing her knuckles where they had connected with his face.

Ntando's lips seemed to be on fire. They began to swell immediately and he was spitting blood in the water. As he tried to climb out of the pool, she kicked him in the ribs and he fell back in again. 'Apologise first.'

Amahle stood there, frozen. She looked from him to Samu. Her lips moved but no sound came out. Then she took her clothes and towel, and ran down the stairs of the hotel.

Amahle had no choice but to attend the emergency meeting Ntando had called between their families that Saturday morning. She was in extreme agitation ever since Ntando had followed her like a stalker and confronted her at the hotel. Samu had tried to call her after that incident, but Amahle could not talk to her. She had not been brave enough to confirm or deny anything about her sexual preference to her fighting lovers. How was she going to do that in front of her conservative, traditional family? Her stomach was aching with fear. She would have to find courage somehow. She knew Ntando's aim with the meeting was to call their marriage off, and to claim back his first lobolo instalment that he had paid a year ago. Twelve cattle, to be precise.

The meeting was held at Amahle's hostel home in Soweto where she had been staying since Ntando had caught her cheating. Her family, who was originally from Ixopo in KwaZulu-Natal, was in attendance. Ntando's mother and uncles had come all the way from Greytown. In their eyes, the two of them were as good as married.

Amahle's mother had prepared umqombothi beer and slaughtered a few chickens for the guests. The calabash of beer was being passed around among the men even before the matter was brought forward. Ntando's aunt, the chief negotiator, was there too. She was a woman of about seventy years of age, erect, keen of eye and without a tooth missing in her mouth.

Amahle had taken up a position against the door. She did not look Ntando in the eye. Her hand played with a piece of cloth, an old favourite blanket of their six-year-old son when he was a baby that had been washed thin and torn. With the back of her fingers, she caressed it.

Ntando's uncle, Mgiliji, hung his hat on his knee and propped his stick against the wall before introducing what brought them to the Gasa family. His left eye was a little smaller than his right, and had a tendency to blink, a minor flaw.

'The Cele family were asked to come solve the matter between our two children whom we love, Ntando and Amahle. Apparently, the two are no longer at peace with each other, hence they are no longer living together.' Mgiliji's mind was lucid and he was speaking coherently. 'We have come here to establish the peace, if possible, between the young husband and wife. But we can only do that if we know in detail what happened. First, we would like to hear what had happened to make my nephew take the decision he took. Ntando, the floor is yours. Then we will hear from our makoti, and make deliberations.'

'Last week, I caught my wife cheating on me at the Parktonian Hotel.' Ntando was peering intently at her. There was a slight shrinking, a diminishing in his assurance. He paused, as if not sure whether he should use a whining voice that would play for sympathy.

'Cheating with whom?' interjected Amahle's uncle, who was sitting with her mother at the other end of the room. 'Do you know the person, by any chance?'

'Well, it was with another lady called Samu,' Ntando said, his voice slow. 'I don't know where she is from. But it seems she is from around Joburg according to the way she sounds when she speaks.'

Amahle tried to say something but could not get her mouth open. A strange pain hit her between the eyes. If she were to confess, she would start sobbing.

'That's not the truth,' she said after a long pause, looking at the floor. 'Samu is just my friend who was trying to get me a job where she works at the Parktonian. I tried to explain to him and he could not believe me.'

She could not bear looking those old people in the eye. It was not because she feared that the lying mask on her face would be torn off, but rather because she was afraid of betraying herself.

'Wait, mshana, you say you caught makoti cheating with another woman?' asked Uncle Mgiliji.

'Yes, I caught them kissing at the hotel pool.'

They were all silently looking at Ntando, as though silence belonged and had always belonged to them.

His uncle was shaking his head. 'What kind of nonsense is this?' His incisors sank into his lower lip. 'Are you mad in your head?

You mean you brought us all the way from KwaZulu because you think your wife is in love with another woman. Where have you heard such nonsense? Look at your wife.' He pointed towards Amahle and she glanced up at him quickly. 'She is a full-blooded woman. Does she look like a man? She is as feminine as they come. Don't embarrass us like this with the Gasa family again. Next time you must get your facts right.'

Ntando's head went into that gesture she loved, which was partly a nod, partly a possible disagreement. When he looked up again, his eyes were watery. He was staring at her and she looked away.

'Tell them the truth, Amahle. Maybe I will forgive you.'

'It's not the truth,' she answered in a muffled tone, hating herself for the self-denial but not able to do anything else. 'Samu is just a friend.'

Everyone looked at Ntando and slowly shook their heads.

'Then why did you run away after I caught you?'

'You were embarrassing me in front of my friend, just like you are embarrassing me in front of the elders.' She paused. 'I was not lying to you the other day when I said I loved you. I still do love you a lot, but you have become possessive and full of obsession. It scares me that you have developed this kind of insecurity.'

She was surprised by her own words. She couldn't stop herself. Her mouth was saying whatever it needed to allay the unanswered questions, the blank stares, the silence.

With shaking hands, Ntando tottered to his chair as if it were all too painful for him to handle. 'Stop lying, Amahle.'

His uncle Mgiliji was now doing the talking, and emphasised his words with his hands.

'We find what my nephew is saying not only childish, but embarrassing.' He slammed his hands together as if killing an imaginary fly. 'If I knew, I would not have wasted my time coming here all the way from KwaZulu-Natal. It is clear he has forgotten who he is talking to. Of course every man has a burning curiosity to see the person who has taken his place in his wife's heart. But today I'm shocked to hear that my nephew thinks a woman can steal a man's wife. If that were true, he would not be a real man. It is clear that our son is imagining things. Where I come from, I have never seen a man say a woman has taken his wife. He is embarrassing us.'

Her uncle smiled and shook his head. 'Thank you for the wise words, Ndosi. Those are the words that strengthen our relationship. It is clear that your nephew has misinterpreted his wife's behaviour by assuming things. That he is capable of formulating such nonsense in his mind surprises and troubles me. He must not play with our child's love. She will leave him for real in the future.'

'Makoti, we admire you for your honesty and strength,' said Ntando's aunt to Amahle. 'We still need to teach your husband that a man's day must begin with the pleasure of lifting his eyelids to see his wife sleeping next to him. We will definitely fix things with our son. Ntando, you have to apologise to your wife, too.'

'We are concerned about our son-in-law,' Amahle's uncle said. 'If he is capable of crowding his brain with such strange thoughts, it means he is also capable of manufacturing imaginary enemies against his own family. He will end up destroying his family.'

'We understand your concerns. It is genuine. What we will do is to perform some rituals for him. After exorcising him, we will come back for our makoti.'

When Amahle dared glance at Ntando again, he was frowning at her in disgust. 'Looks like you won, dear wife,' he said.

Amahle was left wondering what, exactly, she had won.

FIREPLACE

MEC Comrade Leadership Mgobhozi and his former driver, now businessman Comrade Vuyani, were counting the money that Comrade Vuyani had brought to Mgobhozi's Shandon Estate mansion that cold Saturday morning. Mgobhozi sat at the oak dining table in his spacious home with his pen between his teeth as he flipped through the banknotes. Then he took out the pen, made calculations and wrote them down in a little black notebook.

Comrade Vuyani, who was sitting across from Mgobhozi, had worked as his driver and bodyguard for seven years. He'd resigned about a year ago on the advice of Mgobhozi himself and started a company called Go Transport. A week after the company was registered, it was awarded a lucrative ten-million-rand tender to offer transport services for school children in the Mpumalanga area of Bushbuckridge near the Kruger National Park. A percentage of the tender money had to go to Comrade Leadership Mgobhozi, who had pulled strings to make sure that it was awarded to Go Transport. The first instalment of that percentage was what Mgobhozi and Vuyani were counting now.

Just the previous month, Mgobhozi's other former driver, Comrade Mzamo, was awarded a fifteen-million-rand tender to fix the potholes around the Kanyamazane area. MEC Comrade Leadership Mgobhozi also got his cut from that tender.

'So, Leadership, I guess I will see you next week to pay you the next instalment,' said Comrade Vuyani as he wiped his nose with his hand.

Mgobhozi avoided Vuyani's eyes and looked closely at the fire, which was burning in the fireplace. He was beside himself with excitement. He jotted another note, laid down his pen and softly laughed to himself. Winking, he continued counting the money.

'Not next week, Comrade Vuyani,' answered MEC Comrade Leadership while holding a bundle of two-hundred-rand bank-notes. 'Do you want to look suspicious to the authorities? I must teach you this game properly. You can't withdraw such huge amounts of cash week after week. The bank and the police will start following you wherever you go to see who you deliver your black plastic bag to.'

'I'm sorry, I overlooked that possibility.'

'Don't worry, Comrade. I know you are still new to this game. It is my responsibility to teach you.' He paused and looked at Vuyani. 'Do you by any chance watch the National Geographic channel, Comrade?'

'Well, sometimes, yes.'

'You must watch it, Comrade. Then you will learn a lot about the law of the jungle,' Mgobhozi said as his eyes concentrated on the leopard on the two-hundred-rand bill. 'Do you know what lesson we can learn from the leopard?'

'No, Comrade Leadership. Please tell me.'

'The law of the jungle is such that it is not enough for a leopard to teach its cubs how to hunt. It must also impart knowledge on how to carry what it has killed up the tree. Otherwise, the cubs may not enjoy their food with the hyenas and the jackals around. So, it is my responsibility to teach you how to enjoy your money in peace without the nuisance of the police and the journalists. Take my advice. Don't come next week, Comrade. Besides, I'm going on a holiday with my wife.'

Mgobhozi got up and walked a short distance around the room. His stomach wobbled and preceded him. He slightly envied the more youthful, toned body of Vuyani, but other than that, he knew he was the one to be envied. Mgobhozi lived in a home with ten bedrooms, all of which were en-suite for maximum privacy. Other features of the house included walk-in dressing rooms, a kitchen, scullery, pantry, entertainment area with jacuzzi, bar, braai area, as well as a patio leading onto a heated pool with a lush green garden on the far side of it. There was also a wine cellar, additional accommodation for childminders and a VIP security team, and even a helicopter pad in the huge yard, although Mgobhozi had never owned a helicopter.

'Oh, I didn't know you're going on holiday? Where are you headed, Comrade Leadership?'

'We are going on a trip around the world basically: New York, Rome and Dubai.'

Mgobhozi was aware of Vuyani's glance, which lingered admiringly on the purple Gucci jacket he was wearing. On his wrist he wore an eighteen-carat yellow gold Rolex Cosmograph Daytona, which featured a bezel set with thirty-six cognac baguette sapphires and a dial with the image of a leopard on it. It had cost him over a million rand.

'Life is good, Comrade Leadership. I guess sometimes it's important to have a little fun. When you come back from those places, you will have new ideas and new focus to help lead the people.'

Mgobhozi nodded. He brushed fictional dust from the shoulder of his jacket. Not a minute passed without his consciousness of the new Gucci jacket he was wearing.

'Do you still remember what I said to you before you registered your company? I told you that money only comes to those who are willing to spend it. You can't always be wearing that serious businessman look. Life is too short, Comrade Vuyani. You have to smile. Don't forget to have a little fun.'

'I know, Comrade Leadership.' He paused. 'You and your wife must enjoy yourselves. I would love to go to New York one day. But it is too expensive.'

'What do you mean, *it is too expensive*? You have just received a ten-million-rand tender.'

'I know, but I have lots of bills to pay. Besides, I must still give you your full thirty per cent cut of the tender.'

'Who doesn't have bills to pay? Stop being a miser, Comrade Vuyani. Once or twice in a month you must loosen up and allow your body to behave foolishly by spending. Just like children behave foolishly and pointlessly, for the sake of a little fun. You and I can afford that luxury. You must buy nice clothes, beautiful prostitutes, cars and airplane tickets to anywhere in the world.'

'Maybe next year I will be able to travel.'

'This thing is simple, Comrade Vuyani.' Mgobhozi lowered his voice to impart his secret to being successful. 'Rich politicians like us must also be entertained in order to lead the people.' He paused and touched the zip of his trousers. 'It is the duty of the taxpayers to always foot our bill. Whether they like it or not, complain or not, it is their duty to make sure I lead with a happy soul. That is the way the world is.'

The two men laughed at this. Mgobhozi felt that it was his duty to stay close to Vuyani so that Vuyani could benefit from him and absorb his knowledge, instead of groping his own way laboriously towards it. They had been friends since high school. Mgobhozi knew Vuyani as often lost and uncertain.

Shaking his head, Mgobhozi looked at Vuyani. 'We are not born equal in this world.'

There was a look of acceptance in Vuyani's eyes. 'You think so, Comrade Leadership?'

'Yes, Comrade. Inequality is all over the world. Even education systems have a surprising unequal outcome, Comrade. You know why?'

'I'm not sure I'm following what you're saying.'

'Okay, let me break it down for you. Picture this simple practical example. Let's go back to our school in Bushbuckridge. The cleverest student, for example, passes his matric with first class, just like that guy we went to school with, Xolani. He gets admission to the best medical and engineering schools like Wits University and UCT. The second-class student, like that lady, Bobo, is also admitted to do an MBA or LLB. In this scenario which I have painted, do you see that it is obvious that the second-class student is destined to manage the first-class students with his or her MBA and LLB? You follow me, Comrade Vuyani?'

'Yes, Comrade Leadership, I follow you.'

'Okay, let's look at the third-class high-school students – that is you and me, Comrade Vuyani. We entered politics to govern the first-class and second-class students. Those are students like Bobo and Xoli who are doctors, engineers, lawyers and managers of big companies today. We tell them what to do and not do in their qualified fields even if we don't know jack shit. You know why?'

'I guess it's because we are politicians.'

'You're partly right. It's because we are politicians and we have the power. For example, we tell doctors which medicines to use and engineers which roads to build and where, and which cement to mix. We tell big companies how much tax to pay, whom to do business with, and whom to employ in their companies. We also tell them whom to fire from their companies irrespective of whether they are good workers or not. Are you with me, Comrade?'

'Yes, Comrade Leadership. I'm with you.'

'Let me give you another example. Just a few years ago we had Comrade President Mbeki, who told qualified doctors that their antiretrovirals were shitty medicine that would not stop the spread of HIV. What happened next? He stopped its rollout. What did the doctors do? Nothing. And those doctors are the first-class students I'm talking about. They knew from science that a lot of people would die from the spread of HIV if the rollout did not happen. That's the power of us third-class students who become politicians.'

'I'm with you, Comrade Leadership.'

'But that's not all, Comrade Vuyani. The most dangerous group is called high-school failures. This is the group that joins the army and police force to control us politicians. You must be careful with this group. If they are not happy with us politicians, they can kick us out of office or kill us.'

Vuyani's eyes were large and round. He gave a low whistle.

'You see what I mean? Best of all is that those who did not even go to school at all, like your Bushiris and Sosobalas, become prophets and witchdoctors. And your masses, educated or not, follow them religiously.'

Mgobhozi watched Comrade Vuyani as he shifted uncomfortably. He was aware that Vuyani was a staunch supporter of Prophet Bushiri. Comrade Vuyani looked into Mgobhozi's eyes, as if trying to read him and figure out the flow of his thoughts. Vuyani got up from his chair, then took a step backwards with a smile of near disbelief.

'Hayi, Comrade Leadership. I partly agree with you that some people have been given more than they deserve by life, while others have been deprived. That's what our prophet always teaches us. But, Comrade Leadership, we also need to make sure that the people enjoy their freedom and democracy.'

Mgobhozi nodded enthusiastically, as if delighted by this unexpected caution and prudence. He stared fixedly at the oak whisky cabinet in the corner of the room without ceasing to smile at what was being said to him by Comrade Vuyani. As soon as Vuyani had finished talking, Mgobhozi waved his hand in the air, half in contempt, half in satisfaction.

'Don't tell me about voters. Those people are like ants. All they ever do is live for their work and pay tax for us politicians to buy new shoes that we wear to trample on them. You need to change your mindset, Comrade Vuyani. I'm more experienced than you in this game. I want you to adopt and understand my reasoning at a deeper level and accept it as the truth.'

'But last week we both agreed with the Premier when he warned that our noble liberation movement has been hijacked by the tsotsis. He said that there are thugs who use their struggle credentials for self-enrichment through corruption, nepotism and collusion with third parties to defraud the state. I think we must be very careful, Comrade Leadership.'

'Stop fooling yourself, Comrade Vuyani. That's the nature of politics. It often changes colour just like the chameleon. Democracy and freedom are often self-deception among the people.'

'What do you mean, Comrade?' Vuyani sat down again.

'Let me break it down for you. You take two comrades into power who were sworn enemies, say, Malema and Zuma. Put those two in one room for ten minutes. You know what will happen?'

'Those two hate each other.'

'No, Comrade. They are not going to kill each other, if that's what you think. They'll not talk about democracy and freedom either. They will instead figure out how to be friends again and swindle the state resources. What I mean is this: You will never be a good politician if you are a man with conscience and goodness. If you are afraid of fire, you must never enlist as a fireman. It is as simple as that. You will burn.'

The counting of the money was done; the meeting was over. Mgobhozi smiled with pleasure as he walked Comrade Vuyani to his car. He walked with a limp, which he'd sustained the night he was thrown off a balcony because of cheating with a married woman. Manto was her name. The highly publicised incident had happened about six years ago when he was still in charge of the

Provincial Department of Refugees, Tourism, Asylum and Displacements. Mgobhozi had since been married twice.

Outside, it was chilly and windy – the kind of wind that was strong enough to carry away the hats of the tsotsis on the streets and mess up beautiful black women's expensive Brazilian hair pieces. On each side of Mgobhozi's long driveway, the tall trees almost hid the road that led to the main gate. The trees twisted as though the cold wind were tickling them. The grass had been freshly cut by the gardener. Its scent travelled upwards. The flowers flashed bright smiles as Mgobhozi walked Vuyani to his black Mercedes.

Vuyani lifted his face to the cold air. His hand trembled a little as he grasped Comrade Mgobhozi's shoulder.

'I guess I will see you when you come back from your travels. Have a safe trip, Comrade Leadership.'

'Thank you, Comrade. I hope you understood my point earlier. Don't be like the masses who complain about everything.'

'I understood everything, Comrade Leadership.'

'Just wait and observe, Comrade. The masses complain to us leaders about useless things. When the weather is hot and dry, they come to us to complain how the heat dries and shrivels their skin. They grumble over the wind that rattles their doors and breaks their lips. They protest against the potholes, even when they don't have cars like us. Those are the masses. And they expect us politicians to listen to that nonsense every day.'

'I know people can be irritating sometimes.'

'Irritating is an understatement. They are a nuisance, sublime nincompoops. My motto is: If I listen, the masses must foot the bill. That's why I asked if you watch the National Geographic channel. From it you will learn why it is important to treat the masses as though they were parrots.'

'Well said, MEC Comrade Leadership. Now please accept my thanks for your kindness, and farewell. Please say bye to your wife for me. I will see you when you come back.'

'Remember that we are the revolutionaries. We are wise. We are politicians at the end of the day. Politicians can be right and still get into terrible fights with the voters. That's because there are so many different ways of being right in politics.'

'I will,' Comrade Vuyani said as he got into the car. 'It's cold out here today. Let's talk soon, Comrade Leadership.'

Mgobhozi watched Vuyani slowly reverse the car down the driveway. This was not the only property Mgobhozi owned. As MEC for Roads and Transport, he had used his position to amass millions of rands through government tenders. He had bought several houses and farms across South Africa.

Before Vuyani drove off, Mgobhozi took a few quick steps to catch up to the car and talked to him through the open window.

'This is the economics of politics, Comrade Vuyani. There is nothing we can do about it. It is like an unavoidable circle of life where we buy our lives with the lives of others.'

As he turned back to the house, Mgobhozi's cellphone rang. The screen registered *private number*, but the voice on the other end was familiar. It was Inspector Kuzwayo, his informant at the Hawks office.

'Yes, Comrade?'

'Comrade Leadership, I suggest you get rid of the money that Vuyani gave to you now. I've just been reliably informed that he works with the Hawks. He has been under investigation for some time.'

'Comrade Vuyani? No way. What do you mean?'

'Do exactly as I say, or you will spend years in jail.'

'This is unbelievable. How come you didn't warn me before?'

'I also just found out less than an hour ago from my colleague at the Hawks, Mr Mbule. He told me that there is a rumour that you are to be used as a sacrificial lamb by the highest powers in the Movement.'

'What do you mean exactly?'

'There is no time to explain, Comrade Leadership. The Movement has decided to use you as an example to deal with serious cases of corruption.'

'This is bizarre and shocking. How do I get rid of one metre in cash?'

'Don't ask me. I don't know. But the Hawks will be there in less than an hour. They are not far from your house. For your information, all those banknotes that Vuyani just gave you are marked and recorded.'

'Why me? I'm the one who delivered the elections to our Premier and the President in the last election campaign,' he said, feeling nauseous. 'If it were not for me, the Movement would have lost this province, let alone the whole country. In fact, the President should get on his knees and sweep the dust from my Gucci shoes with his eyelashes just to thank me for my hard work.'

'It is what it is, Comrade Leadership Mgobhozi. I heard you

are being sacrificed because of what I have warned you about in the past.'

Mgobhozi was now inside the house and staring at the black plastic bag full of cash on the dining-room table. He trotted to his oak whisky cabinet and poured three fingers of his expensive Blue Label whisky in a glass. He hoped it would lighten his suddenly low spirits and he swallowed it in one go as though it were some unpleasant medicine. It did not help to uplift his state of mind.

'What exactly did you warn me about in the past?' Mgobhozi barked at Inspector Kuzwayo who was still on the other end of the line.

'You know exactly what I mean, Comrade Leadership. I told you to stop chewing the centre of other Comrades' wives and girl-friends within the Movement. That thing has come back to haunt you. Everyone hates you for that because it is unrevolutionary. I also warned you that our deputy at the Hawks has not forgiven you for sleeping with his wife in Alberton, that time when he threw you from the balcony. Do you remember him?'

'You mean that nincompoop Dumi has something to do with this?'

'It seems like it.'

'But everyone, including the President, knows that this money is to be used for the next local election campaign for the Movement. Why would they want to implicate me alone for corruption?'

'But that's not the reason why they want you brought low, Comrade. The centre is your downfall, as I warned you a long time ago. You love the centre too much. I told you it will make you lose focus, and you will die, Comrade. The centre kills. Remember the words of the Premier when we visited him? He warned us that the lips and the penis of a foolish comrade are his ruin. That is what is coming back to bite you.'

'Why do they single me out?'

'You gave them the sword with which to stab you in the back, Comrade Leadership. Just be careful. The centre is too dangerous. The centre corrupts. I warned you previously that one day things will fall apart. The centre will not hold.'

'Why are people jealous of another black man's success? Sell-outs. White monopoly capital agents!'

'Listen, Leadership. You don't have time. You cannot even go out of the house now. Your movements are being monitored as we speak. Don't worry, I'm using our secure line. But your enemies are too numerous in our beloved organisation. The dangers confronting you are from every penis-owner and phallic-obsessed princess. It's too unpredictable, Leadership.'

'I wish someone could tell this Premier and President who are now after me that it is very bad manners to speak about corruption while they are eating, too. I will expose them. We have files of their kids eating with their mouths open. On top of this, we know that some of these people were apartheid spies in the past. These are the same people who claim that apartheid was better than corruptheid.'

'Do it quickly – get rid of the money, Comrade Leadership, before the Hawks arrive at your door any moment now.'

The line went dead. Comrade Mgobhozi tried to call the number again, but a woman's voice said, 'The number you dialled does not exist.' Mgobhozi rolled his head back and looked at the ceiling.

It came to his mind that most people in the Movement derogatively called him a 'gynaecologist' behind his back because he liked sleeping with all those young girls with short skirts and tight blouses.

Mgobhozi sat down on the couch by the glow of the fireplace. He felt a light itch at the top of his belly and slid a little closer to the fire. With his cellphone still in his hand, he tried to phone the Premier of the province. To his disgust, the Premier's phone went to voicemail. He remembered the Premier's words that 'the country's collapse was paining the President's soul, as if it were an actual organ with blood flowing through it'. The leader of the Hawks was now Dumi, whose wife, Manto, Mgobhozi had once cheated with. He'd narrowly escaped death after Dumi found the two of them cheating.

'What do they know about the centre?' he said to himself. He got up and poured another glass of whisky at his drinks station. 'Fuck them. Why is it my problem if their girlfriends and wives are like used bicycles that are ridden and exhausted by the entire Movement manhood?'

He paused and searched for big words in his brain. He had a reputation for bluntness when angry. Finding no suitable words, he coined a lot of untranslatable new ones.

'What msunery is this? This is fuckology. Bloody sellouts. Nincompoops. Morons. Buffoons. These political midgets are trying to be heroes of the masses by treating me like their used political condom. Never! They don't know me. I will show them that their so-called heroism is a dangerous kind of stupidity.'

He took quick steps back to the couch and threw himself down on it while still holding his whisky glass in his left hand and his cellphone in the right. As he did this, he saw his wife, Tiyandza, come down the stairs from their top-floor bedroom, carrying her MacBook Pro. He tried to force a smile as he watched her walk on the balls of her feet. She was wearing a very short blue dress. It was so tight that it accentuated the shape of her firm breasts and her broad hips. She came towards him with wide strides. When she placed the weight of her body on either the right or the left foot, her buttocks swayed in the opposite direction. She sat down across from him on the other couch and perused her laptop. Mgobhozi kept staring at her, unsmiling. He could see enjoyment in her face.

'Baby, I found this hotel in Venice. You will love it,' Tiyandza said, her body quivering with joy. 'I booked the New York hotel, too, and a trip to Niagara Falls. We will be staying at the Marriott Fallsview Hotel & Spa.'

It was amazing how a fifty-nine-year-old man allowed himself to be called 'baby' by a twenty-four-year-old woman. Of course Tiyandza's beauty gave her that licence. Their world was good and simple, and Mgobhozi was delighted with their happiness. He loved how her suggestive stride and oscillating hips sent men into reveries of infidelity. Her breasts were firm like green Limpopo avocadoes. Tiyandza was his fifth wife. They'd married about seven months ago, but essentially Mgobhozi was a bachelor at heart and in character. He didn't believe in permanence, in relationships that spanned years. But with Tiyandza, he was willing to try it. During the process of their bitter divorce case, his previous wife, Linda, had called him a stubborn, arrogant and low-life bastard.

She had called him a good-for-nothing, fat and ugly man who cared about no one but himself.

Mgobhozi thought about what his new wife had just said. His head was inclined to the side, and he was sadly searching her eyes. 'Cancel it. We're no longer going.'

The words startled Tiyandza so much that she stood up, threw the laptop on the couch and took a step back. Then she cupped her hands around her mouth.

'What are you saying? What happened, baby? I have already made all the necessary bookings.'

Mgobhozi banged the back of his head against the wall in determination and fury. He felt sharply the betrayal of their friendship by Comrade Vuyani.

'Apparently the Hawks are on their way to arrest me. We must get rid of the money on the table now.'

'But why do they want to arrest you? Is it because of the money?'

'It's politics, babe, not money per se. Politics is like a ghost. It always comes back to haunt the leadership. I have waited two decades before being allowed in through the front door of the Movement. But now it seems the people I put in power are trying to kick me out.'

'This is not fair. You have done a lot for the people.'

'The first rule in politics is that there are no permanent friends and there are no permanent enemies. We only serve our permanent interests.'

He looked at her again without a word. He could see how shaken Tiyandza was. It was as if she had been allowed to glimpse a treasure and then told to abandon it. She had already told her friends and colleagues that she was going away. Mgobhozi had heard her talk to friends and relatives on the phone while planning the much-anticipated trip. During those loud conversations, he had heard her promise people she would bring back gifts from overseas.

'Aw,' she groaned. 'I can't believe this. I really can't.'

Mgobhozi looked at Tiyandza as she sat down on the couch again and stared at the ceiling. For a few moments, her eyes were transfixed by one particular spot by the lights. Her face crumpled and tears gathered in her eyes. She bit her quivering lower lip.

'Are you okay, babe?'

'Are they coming to arrest me, too?'

'Arrest you? What for?'

His half-opened lips produced a bubble of saliva. It burst when he breathed out. He went over to his wife and pulled her up from the couch to give her a hug.

'I don't know,' she said as she softly pushed him away. 'Maybe because of the money you took? They will think I'm also involved.'

'They will not arrest anyone if I get rid of the money.'

'Get rid of the money?'

'Yes, babe, this is just a temporary inconvenience. We will make some more, don't worry.'

Mgobhozi focused on Tiyandza's long nails as she sat down and began to scratch her forehead. Seconds later, she was sprawled, half sitting and half lying, across the length of the couch.

'How? I mean, how are we getting rid of such a huge amount?' She pointed towards the black plastic bag on the table. 'Do we put it in the safe?'

'We can't do that, babe. The money is marked. If they find it,

I'm finished. We will have to burn it over there,' he said, pointing at the fireplace. 'In that way, there is no evidence and we won't be implicated.'

He watched Tiyandza purse her lips in a mixture of scepticism and vague annoyance. Mgobhozi bowed his head, embarrassed. He then removed his jacket and unbuttoned his shirt. In a gesture quite unlike him, he took off his shoes and put his feet on the little coffee table for a short while.

'My problem is this nincompoop called Dumi. He is the deputy of the Hawks now. His displeasure with me, as I clearly see, dates way back. Nothing can remove it. I warned the comrades against putting him in such a strategic position.'

Almost simultaneously, Mgobhozi and Tiyandza both stood up. Mgobhozi retrieved the black bag from the table and put bundles of money into the burning fire. He also threw in the notebook that was on the table. With a suffocating feeling, Mgobhozi watched as the leopard on a two-hundred-rand note was consumed by fire.

As Mgobhozi threw another bundle of money into the fire, Tiyandza shivered to see the cash burn. Mgobhozi watched Tiyandza as she gripped the back of the couch with one hand.

'But, what if the Hawks don't come? What if it was all a joke?'

'There is no joke in politics. They will surely come.'

'Can't we dig a hole and hide the money in the garden? In the movies they hide it inside the fridge or in the ceiling.'

'That's the first place they'll look.'

Tiyandza fiddled with her dress while a tear rolled down her left cheek. Her mouth was half open, but she closed it again without saying another word.

Mgobhozi was overwhelmed with feelings of resentment. Rocking back and forth, he watched the money in the flames before him.

Suddenly, he heard Tiyandza cry out, 'This is not fair!'

He looked at her as she spun round, disorientated.

'Are you okay, babe?'

'I'll be fine,' she said in a low voice, 'but I wish you didn't have to burn our fortune.'

He shook his head pityingly. Mgobhozi followed her with his eyes as she walked away up the stairs to their bedroom. He heard her slam the door.

Mgobhozi continued to burn the money. He watched the fire consume the notes. His mind was on the leopard print as if he were watching a real leopard burning in the jungle. He rocked his head back and forth as he remembered his favourite piece of advice about the leopard that he had told Comrade Vuyani. It was not right to burn such a beautiful animal, he thought with a touch of pity and disgust.

After a while, he stood up drunkenly and went to their bedroom to check on his wife. Normally, she would have opened her eyes when he entered and looked admiringly at him. He paused at the door and saw her head was entirely covered by the comforter. He then went to the window and opened the blinds slightly before leaning his head against the wall. From the window, he could see the Hawks' branded Golf 7 cars. They were visible from afar where the street inclined gently uphill from the estate.

'They're here, babe.'

'What do we do?' she asked, peeking her head out from under the comforter.

'Stay in here. I will deal with them. Don't come out, and don't answer anyone.' He nodded at her, winked affectionately. 'Pretend you're in bed sick.'

Tiyandza nodded her approval.

Without thinking twice, Mgobhozi walked downstairs to the fireplace and put the remainder of the money into it. He retrieved a litre of paraffin that he always used to start the fire and poured a quarter of it into the fireplace. The fire consumed the bundles of two-hundred-rand notes very quickly as the image of the leopard played in his head. He took the empty black bag and stuffed it into a kitchen drawer that contained other refuse bags. Back in the living room, he stealthily peeped through the window and saw the six Golf 7 Hawks cars were already at his gate. He opened the window to let the smell of paraffin out. At the drinks station, he poured himself four fingers of whisky.

A feeling of horror and amazement gripped Mgobhozi when he saw through the window that Dumi was at his gate, pressing the buzzer continuously. With dread, he awaited the calamity about to fall on his head. His chin involuntarily dropped the moment he sat on the couch with his whisky glass in his hand. For a moment, his breath passed feebly from his nostrils.

'Open the gate or we will break it down,' Dumi's voice said from the speaker. His voice was not loud, but persuasive and arresting.

Mgobhozi allowed himself to remain seated on his couch for a good while. He lay down on his back, his eyelids shut, feeling the fire warm his bones. He drained his whisky in a single gulp, wiping his mouth with the back of his hand.

At this point, Dumi and his Hawks team seemed to lose their temper. 'We will call the task force in two minutes and you will regret your foolish action.'

Mgobhozi experienced a brief moment of dejection, weakness and disorientation before once more thinking calmly.

Within minutes, the electricity supply to his house was cut. He heard his main gate being lifted off its rails.

Looking at his fireplace, he was satisfied to see the last bits of notes being turned into black ash. His mind registered a black leopard sleeping somewhere by the fireplace. These thoughts were interrupted by Dumi, shouting orders at the front door.

The door was flung open. Mgobhozi roared in rage the moment Dumi and his team entered. Dumi's eyes took in the sitting room before he looked at Mgobhozi. They then swept across him like a radar. Four officers had entered with Dumi. He leaned towards a white female officer and whispered something to her while the officer nodded.

'Happy looters' day, MEC Comrade Leadership Mgobhozi,' said Dumi mockingly. 'Why didn't you open your gate on time?'

'I was not expecting any visitors.'

'You know you can be charged with obstruction of justice for that?' Dumi looked in happy expectation of some great victory for the Hawks.

'Charged for what? For not opening my gate? Please go ahead.'

Dumi dismissed his comment with a wave of his hand.

Two of the five officers stood close to the fireplace and kept rubbing their hands, absorbing the heat. Dumi looked at the officers before giving them instructions. His impersonal gaze flitted from one officer to another without dwelling on any particular face.

'Start searching the house. Mawila and Nyathi, you start here.' He had the Zulu habit of calling people by izithakazelo and surnames. 'Nel and Naidoo, go upstairs. Go through everything – his clothes, everything. Rip his bed apart if necessary. Inspector Mawila, please tell Maake and Midzi outside to check every corner of the house and use the sniffer dog. They must dig at suspicious spots, starting at the swimming pool.'

Mgobhozi looked at Dumi and the officers with irritation. He blamed himself for failing to predict the wholly predictable eventuality that Dumi would at some stage present himself, in person, just to humiliate him.

'What do you want? Where is your warrant to search my house?'

'Relax, we have the warrant.' Dumi winked and produced a diabolical roguish laugh.

Notebook in hand, his female colleague Nel jotted things down as she walked about the room. She opened drawers, looked at her notes, made comparisons, and wrote some more. The skin on her face was glowing and smooth, and she was almost beautiful when she smiled. Then she headed upstairs with her colleague, Naidoo.

'You know exactly what we want,' said Dumi to Mgobhozi. 'Where is the money that Vuyani delivered to you this morning in a black plastic bag?'

'I don't know what you're talking about,' replied Mgobhozi, pretending to be indignant. 'Who lied to you by claiming that Comrade Vuyani gave me money?' He laughed a bit to soften the edge of scorn that was evident in his voice.

Dumi was unapologetic. 'No need to tell us now. We will speak about that once the search is complete. You will tell us the truth then or on your way to jail.'

'The country we live in today is a strange world. It is a world in which some things matter more than your truth.'

Dumi's eyes had a look of pride, triumph and self-assurance that put Mgobhozi slightly on his guard.

'Don't worry. We will find the truth soon.'

'The truth is very often overrated. Just like the fire there, it has the potential to warm us or to burn us. But very soon the same fire will be ashes.'

'You will speak your stupid philosophy in jail with other corrupt criminals. Nothing lasts forever in this world, Mr Mgobhozi. That job you're abusing will end soon – today, actually. When you go to prison, you'll regret everything. You must stop wasting our time and tell the truth. We know Vuyani gave you the money. Don't make this hard on yourself.'

'In politics there is no one truth. We have versions of truths. What Comrade Vuyani told you was maybe his version of the truth because he is also a politician. Maybe an illusion. I didn't receive any money from him. Feel free to search my house.'

Mgobhozi heard the officers moving about the kitchen without lifting their feet, so that their shoes scraped on the tiles. He heard them opening the stove, the fridge, the cupboards. He had no doubt that they were going through every inch of the premises.

While sitting on the couch, Mgobhozi's chest tightened with a surge of unexpected anger when he heard the clinking of glasses and plates.

'Don't break anything in my kitchen or I will sue you,' Mgobhozi called out. 'Who sent you nincompoops here to break my things anyway?' he said to Dumi. 'People like me scrape up a few crumbs of happiness, and just as I'm about to reach out and grasp them, along come people like you to snatch them away from me.'

No one paid him any regard. From where he was seated, Mgo-bhozi could not move out of the target of Dumi's gaze. He held his hands crossed over his belly and his head tilted sideways thinking about the money he had spent on the kitchen. It had just been refurbished by Weizter Kitchens some few weeks ago. It was now worth about a million, including the Smeg appliances that his wife had newly bought.

At that moment, two members of Dumi's team descended the stairs empty-handed. Dumi turned his head in the direction of the staircase to see the officers as they returned to the sitting room. Spotting Dumi, Officer Nel shook her head. That was enough to catch Mgobhozi's attention. Nel appeared to be the second-highest ranking member of the delegation after Dumi.

'Nothing, boss. But there is one room that we didn't search.'

Dumi shook his head, irritated. He didn't hide his displeasure. 'Why didn't you search there? I thought I asked you to search everywhere.'

The officer's eyes darted around and then were still when she faced Mgobhozi on the couch. 'There is a lady sleeping in one of the bedrooms. We didn't want to disturb her.'

'I don't care. Search that person, too.'

At the mention of searching his wife, Mgobhozi raised his chin. His eyes widened, and nostrils flared. His intention wasn't really to try to catch Dumi's eye, but in a room filled with his enemies, there was nowhere else for him to look. Besides, he was burning with anger. He studied the two officers to find the best match for him. He then approached Nel, who he thought had the most friendly demeanour.

'But why would you go into my bedroom?'

'We're only following instructions, sir.' He was surprised when she responded warmly.

At the same time, Dumi addressed Mgobhozi: 'We are the Hawks. We search everywhere for crime.'

'You people have no respect and no boundaries. Don't you know that a bedroom is an intimate space where humans hide their souls, secrets and vulnerabilities?'

'We are looking for those secrets. Why do you lie to us, Mgobhozi? We know that Vuyani gave you the money this morning. And you have not been out since then.'

'So where do you think the money is? I mean, you're intruding in my house and digging everywhere, including around my swimming pool.'

'You're lying to us. Why do you lie to us?'

'We lie because we are complex beings. Even Vuyani lied to you.'

'How do you know that Vuyani lied to us?'

'Because a lie is a work of art that those who are simple-minded like you can never really master. Vuyani is smart. He told you a beautiful lie with great imagination and elegance. He is a genius.'

Dumi and the officers walked up the stairs towards the room where Tiyandza pretended to be sleeping. Mgobhozi looked at Dumi who kept his hands in his jacket pockets as he walked. It made everything about him taut and stretched. He had a particular upright walk that made him appear dignified. Mgobhozi followed them, trying to enter the bedroom behind Dumi. But Dumi blocked the door with his imposing size.

'This is an abuse of your powers. You guys will regret this. I'm calling my lawyer and I will sue you and your office.'

Mgobhozi hoped Dumi would bow to him and start apologising. Instead, Dumi gave him a cool look, not too hostile, but not too friendly either. He then looked into Mgobhozi's eyes and grinned roguishly.

'Please don't interfere with our work, Mr Mgobhozi. It will have serious consequences.'

'I can't allow you to intimidate me. I will sue you and the state.'

'Be my guest. Of course, here in our country, the first external sign of wealth is usually exhibited through arrogance. This country is turned upside down by people like you, Mgobhozi. The just pay for sinners.'

Dumi ordered Tiyandza out of the room so that they could start with the search. As she came out, the teasing smile with which she'd greeted them transformed into an expression of amazement. At the same time, a fresh surge of anger was swelling up in Mgobhozi, threatening to drown out all rational thought. He paced up and down the corridor, attempting to calm his temper. He watched Tiyandza as she dragged herself away from the room, down the stairs and into the living room. He followed her. Stopping at his whisky cabinet, he poured himself a triple tot of whisky while Tiyandza sat down on the couch. Mgobhozi went over to the window with some of his strength returning. He closed his eyes and sucked in air between his teeth. Dumi followed him to the living room as if to monitor what he was doing.

'I suggest you sit down on the couch like your wife, and breathe deeply to rid yourself of negative energy,' Dumi said to him.

'Only in dictatorships like Zimbabwe do people intrude on your privacy like this and order you to sit down in your own house. This country is indeed going down the drain.'

Mgobhozi watched Tiyandza as she shifted about on the couch, as though it were full of needles. She was looking down at the floor and making a little buzzing sound with her lips. It was the kind of sound she made when she approached uncertainties in life. Then she lapsed into silence.

'Not even God is democratic,' said Dumi. 'He made big animals such as humans like you and me, elephants and cows, and allows us to be bitten by tiny insects such as mosquitoes and ticks. Mosquitoes are themselves eaten by spiders. Ticks are eaten by birds. Power is always unequal. It is what it is.'

The pattering of an officer's feet grew louder in the upstairs passage. The Indian officer appeared at the top of the stairs and made his way down.

'Look what I found in the wardrobe, sir,' said the officer, showing Dumi a stack of two-hundred-rand notes.

Dumi, who had been watching in some trepidation, broke into a relieved smile. Mgobhozi fidgeted on the couch and tapped the floor nervously with his heel.

'This is what I'm talking about!' Dumi's eyes glittered.

Dumi took the banknotes and put them on the dining-room table. He sat down on the chair, taking out a notebook with words and numbers scribbled in it. While comparing the banknotes with what was written there, he was restlessly rubbing his bottom against the chair, which in turn made a squeaking sound against the tiles.

'These are not the notes we are looking for,' he finally said and the chair stopped squeaking. He looked around at the officers standing on the staircase. 'Come on, go search for more. We are running out of time.'

'But that's all we could find, sir.' Nel's voice was tinny, as though coming from a cheap radio. 'We searched everywhere.'

'It can't be. You know there is more.' His voice grew hoarse. 'This does not even amount to six thousand, and the numbers don't correspond. There is no bunker here. It means the money is some-where in the house or garden. Go and look for it.'

The officers walked back up the stairs towards the master bed-room as if there were indeed someone in there who was not to be disturbed. Mgobhozi's anger deepened and he started cursing, letting forth a torrent of obscenities.

'What the fuck is this?' Mgobhozi waved his hands in the air in agitation. 'Fuck you all. You fuckers can't plant your money in my bedroom to implicate me in your corruption scandal. I'm on to you.'

One of the officers stifled a laugh when Mgobhozi accosted Dumi with clenched fists.

'Don't try to start a fight that you cannot finish. Remember the last time?' Dumi said sternly. 'You will regret it.'

'Fuck off out my house now.' Mgobhozi's voice had lost the rough edge from moments before.

Dumi forced a nod, not quite hostile.

Mgobhozi resisted the urge to slap him.

'We will only leave when we have found what we are looking for. The problem we face in this country today is that people who work hard for a decent living are outnumbered by thugs like you, Mgobhozi. The unemployed masses who vote for the Movement do so to make a living. Those who rule the masses like you steal for a living.'

The Hawks searched the property for over five hours. Mgobhozi and Tiyandza felt immensely relieved as they saw the shadow of displeasure that showed between Dumi's eyes. His whole team had by then gathered in Mgobhozi's living room to tell him their findings, which was that their search had been fruitless. Dumi seemed disgusted by his team's report. He could not look at them, levelling his gaze at the window instead.

The misty weather was now thick enough to obscure even the other side of the swimming pool where his team had been digging.

Mgobhozi whistled thinly between his tongue and the roof of his mouth. Dumi sat down on the chair next to the dining-room table again. He faced the window for a long time. Then he flopped back in his chair, and rubbed his eyes.

'Okay, guys, I'm calling off the search.'

'I told you there is nothing to find,' Mgobhozi said. 'Now you and your department will receive the papers from my lawyers.'

That night, Mgobhozi could not sleep. He complained to his wife about his aching joints. With rather distant pity, Tiyandza eyed him as he left their bedroom to go downstairs. He made a fire in the fireplace and sat on the couch watching it. Each time he looked at the flames, he was haunted by the face of a leopard burning in front of him. His nostrils smelled its burning flesh, and he felt fear as though an enormous stone were crushing his chest. A veil of morose anger hung over him. That's when he fetched his laptop and wrote a life-changing email:

> *Dear Mr President and Premier,*
> *The interconnectivity within social media ecologies have been relaying viral moral panic, peddling flames of lies, creating myths, and muddling the reality of my life as a family man. I am a victim of information distortion, voice cloning, sponsored spooking and political sabotage by your office. Digital media, in their hybridity, have been abused by my enemies to blackmail me, but my spirit, like that of a leopard, will never die.*
>
> *Following the recurring disinformation and virilisation of my alleged immoral unions, dispensed through awkward slacktivism, I'm stepping down from your re-election campaign.*
>
> *When destiny is calling you to doom, you can't resist your enemies. Their wishes sound like commands to you. You do everything blindly just to impress them as you continue digging your grave.*
> *Yours in struggle,*
> *Comrade Mgobhozi*

To this day, Mgobhozi's mind is still preoccupied with the leopard that burns on the two-hundred-rand note. He cannot stand a fireplace and a two-hundred-rand banknote in his wallet, especially when he is drunk.

WOMAN TO WOMAN

Today I will tell you all you need to know, MaKhumalo. It all started when a friend of mine, Botho, sent me screenshots of some photos of my husband. Your daughter, Lesego, had put up those pictures on her Instagram profile. I studied them for hours. I analysed her body language, and was convinced that the two were dating.

In one picture she was wearing silver hoop earrings that were as big as bracelets. Her eyelashes were bushy. They gave her a peculiar loveliness that I assume attracted my husband to her. In the second picture she was turned to the side, so that you could see her large breasts sticking out her front and buttocks that were like pumpkins in the back. She wore a blue bondage-tight skirt. Her black heels made her feet look bound, too.

It was the third picture that made me conclude that she and my husband were lovers. I assume it was taken at your son's funeral. My husband attended with his friends. May your son's soul rest in peace. Your daughter, my husband, Thapelo, and his friends were all wearing black. I saw my Thapelo holding a microphone as if he were eulogising. That's when my anger stuck in my throat. He never even came to my father's funeral when he died four years ago. Of course you don't know all this. I'm only telling you woman to woman that it hurts deeply when your husband betrays you like that.

I immediately DM'd your daughter to ask why she had made the picture with my husband her profile picture. To my shock, she replied that he was her boyfriend of three years. Can you believe that? She even told me she was pregnant with his son and that they were going to name him after my husband's own grandfather.

But I guess as Lesego's mother you were also aware of what was going on between them. They seemed to be in a serious relationship that was also approved by you, her parents. At least, that's what I thought at that time.

At Lesego's unexpected revelation, my eyes misted over. My heart started to pound. I then called Thapelo's friend, Neo. I expected him to deny everything. He read my message because the two ticks turned blue, but he never answered me. Anyway, that's what friends do; they protect each other. But how could Neo deny such a level of connectedness between your daughter and my husband?

That evening, I took a slow bath until the skin on my fingers became yellow and spongy. I could not just ignore, repress, and pretend to forget everything. My body felt in permanent pain. As soon as I got out of the bath, I called my mother, and I remember how she tried to comfort me. 'Boipelo, my daughter, you will never know men until you have gone through their drawers, pockets, and cellphones. Cheating like this is exactly what your father did to me thirty years ago when you were just eleven years old.'

'But how could Thapelo do this to me? We have been together for thirteen years and have two wonderful daughters. What did I do to deserve this kind of treatment from him?'

'Do you remember what I said to you a year ago when you complained that he didn't come home? I told you to make sure that you enjoyed your marriage while it lasted. That's men for you. Before you know it, your breasts will droop like mine. Just like your own father did to me thirty years ago, your Thapelo will find a younger version of you, with nicely curved and snugged hips within the embrace of a pair of jeans.'

I first met Thapelo fifteen years ago at Herman's Place, Protea South in Soweto. I was chilling with my friends, Masechaba and Kgomotso. He was without a doubt a handsome man. His forehead was broad and generous. His eyebrows were two crescent moons above each eye, set well apart. It was something I rarely see in handsome men. I could not stop feeling lucky when he offered to buy me a drink. Every fibre in my body was savouring his presence. Since that day, until we married a year later, Thapelo constituted my whole universe. In fact, that was so until your daughter took him away from me.

When I heard about their relationship, I felt as though some parts of me didn't exist. It was as if I had to cut that part out of me. At first, some disturbing trick of my mind convinced me that your daughter never happened. It was as if your Lesego were in fact a lie, a phantom, a dream or a nightmare that had come to me one suffocating, dark night, and when I opened my eyes to the sunlight, she was nowhere to be seen.

But I could not live in delusion forever. When I came to my senses, my bitterness towards your daughter accumulated in my soul each day, like sewage water gathering at an abandoned dam. My mother's words from when I was only eleven kept echoing in my head each time I thought of Lesego in my husband's arms:

'Baby girl, make sure that the man you choose is your own husband.'

'What do you mean, Ma?'

'Don't worry. Someday you will understand me. I just don't want you to wake up one day and realise that you have wasted your time by marrying someone else's husband like me.'

'But Dad is your husband.'

'He was. Not any more.'

I tried to talk to my in-laws about Thapelo's extramarital relationship with Lesego. Instead of them talking to him as I expected them to do, they confronted me with messages that laid the blame on me. Apparently, what I was experiencing was due to my own oversensitivity. It was my personal responsibility. Talking about this makes me feel my aches and pains of that time all come flooding back. I remember there were times I would cry simply because a leaf fell off its tree in our backyard. Every time that happened, I could see your daughter and my husband through the shifting gaps between the leaves. Their falling reminded me how I had been discarded like one of those dry leaves.

I tried on several occasions to ask your daughter to leave my husband alone, but she would not listen. I even asked my friends Masechaba and Kgomotso to threaten her for me. Instead, Lesego chose to insult me. I still have those WhatsApp messages where she said that I had a figure like a frog. She bragged to me that my husband was about to leave me for her because it was difficult for him to make out where my waist started. That hurt me a lot. Anyway, maybe she was right. Compared to her, I had nothing to boast about as far as looks were concerned. In my mind, I could see the evil smile etching itself into her girlish cheek when she said that. That was the straw that broke the back of my infinite patience. To this day, I have no idea how we women can grab each other by the throat over a man.

May I say, however, that my husband had an exaggerated, almost fanatical fondness for your daughter. At some point, I even thought she had given him some muthi.

About three years ago, he suddenly became terribly meticulous about keeping himself clean. What I found ridiculous is that he spent at least three-quarters of an hour rinsing his mouth out every day and using different kinds of toothbrushes. Now that I knew for sure what brought it on – your daughter – all of this filled me with jealousy, malice and a desire for revenge.

One day I found the courage to confront him. It was better for me to get hurt by the truth than comforted by the lie I was already living. That was after Lesego had boasted about her pregnancy on Instagram and that they were planning to get married.

'Is she your lover?' I asked him while showing him our WhatsApp chat. 'Are you indeed going to marry her?'

'Well, it is true that she is pregnant. I'm really sorry about it. But we are not getting married.'

'No, you're not sorry at all. And you are not telling the truth either. If you are, tell her to abort your child.'

He looked crushed. 'Abort the baby?'

'You heard me correctly. That's if you still care about us, our relationship. I can't compete for a man with a twenty-two-year-old.'

143

I screwed up my one eye and was squinting steadily at him when I said that. My twitching nostrils sniffed the air blowing in through our open bedroom window. I could feel my buttock muscles clenching and unclenched. My hips thrusted back and forth with anger. Thapelo kept his head down, as if he were ashamed. I knew he found it difficult to gaze directly at people who mean every word they say, but that day it was a bit different. His tightly pressed lips showed that he was deep in thought. I could tell that he truly loved your daughter. It was not like this with his previous lover, Dipuo. With her, I was sure that he just wanted an orgasm and not conversation, let alone a relationship. With your daughter it was different, MaKhumalo. My husband's appetite for her had not been matched. She had already taken what I thought was mine, and therefore I knew she had to be controlled. As I realised this, I was blinded with the terrible thought of losing what had been mine.

'Are you listening to me, Thapelo?' I said. 'Otherwise I will do it myself. Don't think I'm not capable of doing it. Get rid of that baby, or I will get rid of them both.'

This seemed to rouse and frighten him. 'Please don't do something stupid. Yes, that child was unplanned. That I admit, I was wrong. I apologise profusely. But he has a right to be born. She will deliver him soon, whether we like it or not.'

'You mean you produced a child who means nothing to you? Is that what you are saying? What kind of a lie is that?'

'No, I mean the damage has already been done. We have to live with that fact.'

MaKhumalo, you should have looked into his face and seen the seriousness that gleamed in his eyes when he mentioned your unborn grandson. He was caught off balance by my direct questions, demands and threats. He just stood there, feet apart and knees slightly bent. His head was a little raised and the air was coming and going through his open mouth.

'Why did you do this to me?' I asked him. 'Why did you start an affair with that woman?'

He clicked his tongue and tapped his chin in thought. That was his trademark gesture, meaning he had no idea. His lips trembled.

'Answer me, damnit,' I demanded.

'What do you want me to say, Boipelo? Women like that always happen to you suddenly as a man. You don't plan to have a relationship with them.'

His answer hurt me. It kept hitting on my chest for a minute. I had a bad taste in my mouth. I looked at him and dropped a mouthful of spit on his face. As I hurried out of our bedroom to the kitchen, I could not suppress the feeling of dread that welled up inside me. It was as though I sensed that something evil was going to happen.

I can recall the scene of that fight as if it were a film. I can re-play it as often as I wish on the screen of my memory. I remember this because, from that day on, Thapelo did not sleep at home.

The feeling of foreboding struck me that same night. It was a strange and frightening evil that took hold until the morning.

Unexpectedly, Thapelo's friend Neo sent me a WhatsApp message a week after Thapelo had walked out of our home. He told me that they were chilling at Florida Lake with Thapelo and your daughter. He even told me of the baby shower that my husband planned for your daughter in a few days' time. It sounded like Neo was getting fed up with your daughter. She had been trying to control my husband, telling him when he should and shouldn't spend time with friends. They didn't like that, Neo confessed to me.

When I heard of them hanging out by the lake and the planned baby shower, I immediately wanted the two of them to vanish and dissolve like sugar in water. I don't remember how I got into my car or drove to the lake, but by half past two I got there. I parked my car at some distance and moved towards their picnic spot under the sunny sky. They were all dancing to loud house music. I'd never seen my husband dance before, let alone listen to that kind of music. He always pretended to love what he called 'mature soul music and jazz'. It seemed your daughter already changed him. When I saw her pressing her cheek to his chest as they danced, I clutched my handbag to my side, strangling its straps with my trembling hands. I felt something in the bag press painfully into my flesh and I fished it out.

Lesego was taken by surprise when she opened her eyes and saw my face before the two of them. She dropped her bottle of cider, clawed at my husband's chest, reeled, screamed, and almost fainted. That was after she had seen what was in my hands.

Pointed at them was my husband's gun, which he usually hid in the study in our house. How did it get into my handbag?

I didn't say a word. Beads of sweat had erupted on my brow.

Your daughter yelped, and I saw her arms outstretched towards the gun as if trying to protect my husband.

My hands trembled with the strain as I pulled the trigger. As

146

your daughter fell, I pulled it again, taking down my husband. To be honest, at that very moment, I experienced a certain amount of pleasure. And then the horror of it all set in.

MaKhumalo, I'm sorry about what I did to your beautiful daughter and my husband. In this prison, I am tormented by my memories and thoughts. Some things are still not clear. I blocked out packing that gun. I don't think it was my intention to kill, was it? Day and night, here in jail I have to preoccupy myself with something, anything, to silence the voices in my head. Each breath is like inhaling fire, and I think I'm always weeping. Sometimes I imagine the shit climbing up out of the latrine and into my mouth. I wake up every morning feeling like a river that has lost its source. But I am only able to travel along it in one direction – that of hope. At least here I have learnt that true redemption is when guilt leads to good.

MaKhumalo, I have stolen your daughter's life by killing her, as well as your grandchild's right to be born. For me, jail is a place to bury those harsh memories. As yet, I cannot erase them. But if I could leave this place, I would chain them to this cell and not take them with me. I know that not many people like me are given the opportunity to wear a different skin, but I hope someday that I will be allowed out on parole. I know the family of the victims have a say in this. All I can assure you of is that I understand the depth of the pain I've caused, the blackness of the grief I've brought onto everyone, especially you, MaKhumalo.

GHOST STORY

Kabelo puts his lunch on the table and falls into his chair. He plants the scuffed elbows of his jacket on the table, and shovels bites of pap and vleis into his mouth. Fluorescent lights buzz above him. The morgue is – fittingly – deathly quiet.

Kabelo looks around at the steel drawers in which the bodies are kept, the high windowless walls of this basement-storey facility and the lights overhead. The same view every day. Thank fuck it's Friday. He takes another bite of his food.

After a while, he pauses his munching to take out the bundle of cash from his pocket. He leafs through the notes and sniffs them. All of this money, made over just two days. It is a nice little extra for him. And all because some people are too squeamish or whatever to prepare the bodies of their nearest and dearest for burial. As usual, this Thursday and Friday people arrived to wash and prepare their deceased for weekend burials, but most of them were too distressed to go through with it. That's precisely when he offers his help – at a fee, of course.

Kabelo counts off three hundred rand from his bundle of money. That was for preparing a male corpse. He counts off an additional four hundred. That was for a female. His standard rates. Kabelo counts aloud as he peels off more of the notes. Six hundred rand was for a corpse that was badly damaged, in a drinking-and-driving accident. Those are the ones people hate to look at most – disfigured, sometimes with a limb missing. He can charge whatever he wants for the work on those corpses and people will gladly pay it. The remaining seven hundred rand in his palm was for another damaged corpse. Some might call it taking advantage, he ponders. But, hey, no one is preventing them from doing the job themselves.

His ex-wife called it taking advantage. When their marriage was over, she said he was physically and morally unattractive. What does she know? She also said a beard is never a good idea for such a short man. Kabelo does not care what other people think of him. He knows people in the township derogatively call him 'Kabza the Small'. So what? Fuck them.

Kabelo fingers his money greedily. This is what he cares about – cash. He doesn't mind doing disgusting jobs as long as he gets paid. Yesterday and this morning he dressed and anointed the bodies according to family specifications. One family asked him to cut their deceased's overgrown nails, shave his head, armpits and even pubic hair. He's seen it all; it doesn't faze him. For over seventeen years, he has been working in this morgue. To him, dressing a corpse is like a clothing-shop owner dressing a mannequin with clothes for sale.

Kabelo gets up from the chair. The pap and vleis is making him thirsty. He opens one of the icy pans with a corpse inside. Reaching in, he takes out a six-pack of his favourite Castle Lager from where he stored it next to the corpse.

Self-assured, self-confident, Kabelo is now drinking his Castle Lager happily, diligently. His lips are wet from licking. Back in his chair, he is eating his pap and vleis with concentration and delight. He rubs his protruding stomach and lets out a loud burp of satisfaction.

Someone rings the bell at the door and Kabelo jumps up. It is Lunga, the paramedic from Distress Alert Operations. He is bringing in another corpse. *Ka-ching,* Kabelo thinks. More money for me.

'What have we here?' he asks Lunga.

'Male, foreigner, from Malawi. Had a spaza shop in Protea South informal settlement in Soweto. That's where we picked him up. You'll still have to get his details – full name, passport number. His widow will come do the paperwork. She was too shook up. I just know the guy's name is Chris and his widow is Mona.'

Lunga zips open the bag. A fly escapes out of the corpse's right ear. The guy has had a beating, Kabelo notices. Not a pretty picture. His widow might not be inclined to want to wash his body. Kabelo just hopes she has money.

'What happened?' he asks as he puts on a pair of gloves and pulls out an empty tray. The two of them lift the body onto it.

'This is what I got from the bystanders: Apparently it all started after two children from the same family died two days ago. The father spread the rumour that his children had died from food poisoning. Then, today, a crowd gathered at the spaza shop that belonged to this Chris from Malawi.' Lunga jerks his thumb in the corpse's direction. 'They accused him of selling expired food to their children. Mandla – that's the father of the dead children – and his friend, Anthony, tied Chris's hands and the crowd beat him with all sorts of weapons, including pangas, sjamboks, knobkerries and stones.'

'Sho,' Kabelo makes the appropriate sound of shock, but in fact he is examining the bumps, dents, cuts and bruises that the weapons made to the man's flesh. The wrists were chafed raw from the ropes that had bound them. He looks at all of this with detached curiosity.

'Yes,' Lunga continues, 'that Mandla and his friend were still there when we arrived. They were talking to the police, but I don't think anything is going to come of it. You know, most police are also against these foreigners. And anyway, I can't say I blame them.'

'Hmm.' Kabelo lifts the head slightly to examine the back of the scull. There is a huge hole and caked blood back there – probably the death blow.

'Don't get me wrong,' Lunga continues, 'I'm not saying it is okay to kill a man, but we are tired of these foreigners by now. Yes, they take our women; they take our jobs. On top of that, they take over our businesses. How do they expect us to survive in the country of our birth?' He is working himself into some kind of rage. 'My younger brother has finished matric, but he has been unemployed for two years, while foreigners get jobs and businesses. They don't even pay tax. And they sell drugs to our young people. Like my brother – he is using cheap drugs because of them. Our streets are full of criminals because of that lot. They must go back to their home. Go back to where they came from.'

Kabelo is not at all interested in Lunga's ravings. 'So it was not really about the food poisoning, but about the man being a foreigner?'

Lunga looks startled. 'Well, I wouldn't say that. The crowd was asking where he got his cheap stock. They thought he manufactured it himself with the intent of poisoning their children. One woman said the spaza shop owner deserved to die because he sold her daughter an expired yoghurt the previous week. She was sick the whole week and could not go to school. She thought her daughter was going to die when she took her to the clinic.'

'And what did the widow say?' Kabelo asks suddenly, afraid that she might not come at all if she also believes her husband to be guilty.

'She claims he never sold expired stuff and that Mandla's children didn't buy from their shop recently. She said the woman sprouting the story about the yoghurt was mad.' Lunga thinks for a while. 'But can you believe these foreigners?'

Kabelo closes the tray and walks Lunga out. When he returns, he sees the remnants of his lunch still laid out on the table. Strange red ants that he has never seen in the morgue are crawling all over it.

Kabelo cleans the table, sprays Doom on the ants, and is about to leave and start his weekend, when the bell rings again. A thin, dark woman with big tearful eyes is at the door.

She introduces herself as Sis Mona, here to see her husband Chris's body.

Kabelo tries his best to dissuade her from having anything to do with the body herself, explaining that he can do the honours for a nominal fee.

She refuses, launching into a frantic speech: 'I was there when it happened. Don't you think I know what my husband's broken body looks like? Don't you think I know exactly what they did to him? I can still see it all happening right in front of me. He was standing there in the dusty street, next to what used to be our spaza shop, frothing at the mouth, staggering to his feet, foamy spittle and blood soaking his beard. They surrounded him, hitting and kicking.

'He collapsed on the ground and rolled around as if fighting for air not to leave his lungs. His assailants would not let go and they kept beating him with their weapons. He had no strength with which to scream.'

Her wet eyes gleam under the fluorescent lights as she continues: 'Flies covered his injured hand. They had tied his wrists with such violence that the ropes had torn the flesh and cut off his circulation. The crowd accused him of poison, told us that we don't belong here.

'Someone hit my husband on the back of his head, and he made such awful choking sounds. Blood dripped from the corners of his mouth. He tried to open his mouth, then closed it again without saying a word. His eyes shut; his head fell to the side. He was dead.

'I know what the dead body of my husband looks like, sir. I was there.'

A chill goes down Kabelo's spine as she talks. This woman is even more crazed than other widows he's seen. 'Yes, yes, of course,' he tries to appease her. He has to relent and open the tray for her. But first she needs to fill in the necessary paperwork.

She talks as if to herself: 'To think that Mandla was once a friend of us. We gave him groceries for free. To this day, he hasn't paid us. He drank from our house. I can still hear him say to my husband in that evil voice: *You will die today, and the shop is going to be mine. I have already paid for it by the blood of my two children.* But his children did not buy from us this week. Why would he say it was so? Why would he accuse my husband and kill him? Chris pleaded with him not to kill him. He told Mandla he could have the shop if he would just let him live. How could he have been so cruel?'

She looks up at Kabelo from where she is sitting at the table filling in the form. He wonders if she wants him to give her a reason, but then she goes on:

'They still haven't arrested him or that filthy Anthony who helped him bind my husband's hands. The police will do nothing. They are cowards. When I phoned them to come, they took their place at a safe distance, afraid of the angry crowd. It was only after they fired five shots and the crowd dispersed that they came closer. By that time it was too late.'

When Kabelo opens the tray for her, she cries, her eyes tearing over. With legs apart and arms by her sides, she stands still and stares at the body.

'Oh, my husband, what did they do to you? Why did these bloody stupid people want to chop the hand that feeds them? You are the one who was helping to feed their bloody hungry families.'

Sis Mona bends down and takes the man's cold hand in hers and squeezes it. She keeps asking the same question over and over, as if waiting for the man's broken wrist to unbend, or for his still twisted mouth to speak.

'What kind of human beings are they? They don't respect another person's life. These bloody people live in the small orbit of their stupid thoughts.'

Suddenly Sis Mona leaps forwards as if she wants to lie down next to her dead husband in the cold tray. Kabelo has to grab her by the shoulders and hold her back.

She weeps wildly and painfully. 'They have killed him. And I know who they are. I thought they were his friends. They looted our shop. They took everything from us, including our old plastic chairs. What kind of a country is this that hates so much?'

She shrugs him off and takes her dead husband's hand once more.

Kabelo glances at the clock on the wall and sees it is the end of his work day. He is not staying here a moment longer. It is Friday, for fuck's sake. Purposefully, he pulls Sis Mona's hand from the man's body as though it were a leech.

Kabelo muddles through Monday morning with a babelas left over from the weekend. He is glad when he can eat his pap and vleis for lunch once more. Of course, he adds a few sips from his ice-cold Castle Lager. After ending the meal with his customary belch, he hears, coming from the door, a loud rustling. He stops, looks around, listens quietly and gravely. It actually sounds like a rushing wind, but at the basement level, that is not possible. He leaps up with a quiver of his body. A chair squeaks somewhere in the corner of the morgue. The fluorescent lights flicker as if the bulbs are burning out. It feels like there is a movement everywhere.

All of the lights go out, except one that emits only a low glow. The corridor and the big room hang in darkness, as if in a buried city. It feels like the darkness is creeping towards him, ready to swallow him whole.

Kabelo is sure he hears a ghost say: 'Please get me out of here, I'm suffocating.'

He is so terrified that in an uncontrollable revulsion he runs out and slams the door shut behind him. Without waiting for the elevator, he takes the stairs to the ground floor in record time. Outside, the dry heat is upsetting to him. He arrives panting at the adjacent building that houses Distress Alert Operations. Employees look up, stunned. Briefly, Kabelo notices Lunga in his paramedic uniform among them. Mr Olivier, the manager, comes out of his glass-walled office to see what is happening.

'There . . .' Kabelo finds it difficult to say where anything is at all. The whole building, the street outside, and the city has become so blurred and mixed up in his mind. A jumble of words fall out of his mouth, but even though he knows that it is complete gibberish, he cannot seem to command his tongue to say what he actually wants it to.

'Big ghost. Wide ghost. Tall ghost. I'm a ghost. You're a ghost. We're ghosts,' he says, demonstrating with his hands.

'Where?' asks the manager.

Kabelo throws his arm around the manager and presses his head against his shoulder. He then closes his eyes in a spasm of nausea. He pulls away just in time not to vomit on Mr Olivier's chest, but he heaves into a wastepaper bin instead.

Someone brings him a glass of water and he gulps it down. He can only produce a few monosyllables after this.

'There. We are. No.'

Frustrated that no one understands him, he grabs the manager by his shirt and drags him outside.

Mr Olivier opens his eyes wide and pushes him away once outside. 'Are you drunk, Kabelo?'

The rest of the employees follow them outside. 'Look. There.' He points to the building that houses the morgue. Finally understanding to some degree what Kabelo wants from them, Mr Olivier and a few of the employees go down to the basement level and enter the morgue with him. The lights come back on immediately when they open the door.

Kabelo peers in fearfully, but he can see nothing out of place in the main room. Did he imagine it all? Then he notices the red ants forming strange pictures on the floor.

Kabelo, along with Mr Olivier and his team, nervously follows the ants to the bathroom next door. They find two men lying on their backs, dead.

'Hey, that's the guys from the mob killing on Friday,' Lunga says. Kabelo now sees that he has also come down to the morgue. 'It's that Mandla and Anthony, the same people who killed the guy I brought in just before the weekend . . .'

'What?' asks Olivier, confused. 'How did they get here?' He looks at Kabelo for an answer.

'I don't know either. I don't think they are registered with us.'

The lights go off again. A strange voice comes from the other room: 'Take me home, please. I don't like this place where time passes slowly without a trace.'

'Who are you, and where is home?' Mr Olivier calls out.

'I'm Chris. I'm suffocating inside your cold chamber pan.'

'Are you not dead?'

'Maybe I'm dead. But dying is only disappearing from view.'

'Where is home?'

'Home is where the world is without sound and where the light is an unending thing.' The voice fades as if completely out of breath and then there is silence.

Fearfully, Mr Olivier leads them back into the main room. Kabelo immediately sees that the cold tray where Chris's body was kept for the past three days is open. The body of the bloodied Chris is sitting on the table as if to finish up Kabelo's leftover food. He is naked, surrounded by red ants. Upon seeing them, Chris's body blows its nose and ants come out.

Gauteng's Department of Health officials arrive an hour later together with the CEO of the Gauteng forensic pathology service.

'We followed procedure,' says the manager of Distress Alert Operations. 'Our man, Lunga, who was on the scene, assures me that all the right checks were done: breathing, pulse. That's why we declared him dead. I've never seen anything like this in my thirty years' experience.'

'What about the two other bodies?' an official wants to know.

'We're still investigating that. Perhaps one of my people brought them in while Kabelo, the man who works here, was out. Perhaps they came with a different service. It might have been a mistake. They could have been delivered to the wrong morgue. We're asking around, looking into it.' Mr Olivier opens his palms, then clasps his hands together, as if in supplication.

'What I still don't understand,' another official asks, 'is how could a person with such bad injuries wake up from the dead after three days in a cold morgue pan?'

'As I have said before, my forensic officers collected the body for storage and for further investigations to determine the cause of the death by a pathologist. Then we later found him alive. It's a miracle.'

Mr Olivier takes off his glasses, wipes the lenses clean with his handkerchief.

Behind him, Kabelo and Lunga are standing by the wall. The fingertips of Kabelo's right hand press against the coarse texture of the whitewashed wall, as if that can ground him.

'It's a miracle,' he repeats. 'A ghost.' But it feels more like revenge for wicked deeds meted out by some unknown, all-powerful force. And Kabelo is scared shitless.

THE IN-LAWS

'Why did it have to come to this?' Marang murmurs as she climbs the steps to the court to hear the outcome of her case.

'I hope those are only thoughts and not regrets,' her mother, Kele, says beside her. 'You did well to challenge your in-laws in court.'

Marang nods silently, thankful for her mother's support in accompanying her to court since the whole application started. Her mother and two young children are the only people who have been good to Marang in these difficult times. They have re-inforced her in the view that her life – her person – has meaning and value.

'As a woman, one has to fight,' her mother continues. 'It is almost a virtual moral obligation for every oppressed woman. That is the reason I encouraged you to challenge them. And don't worry, you will win this case.'

Marang is not so sure. She dreads what the day will bring.

In the foyer, they find Marang's in-laws waiting to be let into the courtroom as well. A different case is in session and they all have to wait.

Her brother-in-law, Fakazi, looks at her shiftily, with a mixture of hatred and curiosity. Her eyes meet those of her father-in-law, the old man Ntimani, briefly. He stares at her, then at the inside of the hat in his hand. He taps it, gazes inside again and puts it on his head, his face twisting in a contemptuous scowl. Sadness and resentment rise up in her when she recognises the oversized three-piece navy suit old man Ntimani is wearing. It is the suit that her late husband, Kumani, bought and planned to wear on their wedding day. But he never did because that happy day never happened. She recognises it despite the suit now being shiny from too much ironing. How dare the old man wear it?

Her late husband's two sisters, Rea and Dineo, are gazing at her derisively. They look her up and down, making her feel naked. Their lips are twisted. 'Sies, you witch. Today it will be over for you,' one of the sisters, Rea, says. 'You will not get away with this.'

'Don't bother responding to idiots.' Marang's mother, Kele, puts a reassuring arm around her. 'Their actions are like the last kick of a dying horse.'

Marang keeps quiet and looks ahead stubbornly. She pretends to be unaware of her in-laws' presence. She is immune to the insults by now. But the knowledge that all four of them detest her still brings her immense pain.

Why did it have to come to this? she asks herself again as she replays in her mind the events since her husband's death a few short months ago.

Marang had not yet recovered from the shock of her husband's fatal car accident, of being widowed with two little girls, when she was shaken once again by the sudden realisation that his family had turned on her in her hour of deepest need.

'We will bury him in Bushbuckridge, Mpumalanga,' her father-in-law informed her over the phone.

161

'But he lived in Johannesburg,' she protested. She wondered why she hadn't been consulted but knew she had to stay respectful towards her father-in-law as custom and tradition demanded.

'He will be buried at the family home in Mpumalanga.'

'But I am also his family. His children are also his family.'

He was silent for a while, then said: 'You are not his family and you are not our family. You will not join us for the burial on our ancestral land.'

'But I'm his wife. You all welcomed me when you paid lobolo to my family three years ago. What has changed now?'

He gave a snort. 'Where have you seen a valid marriage where there is no handover of the bride? You must ask your parents to fill those gaps for you so that you can understand what a wife is. If they know our tradition, which I doubt, they will tell you that the handing over of the bride is the crucial part of our customary marriage. It didn't happen with you. So, you are not part of the family.'

'But you paid the lobolo. You were part of the negotiation. I've lived in this house with my husband for three years. What about our children?'

'As far as we're concerned, the children are born out of wedlock because you and my son were not married. You cannot claim anything here.'

Tears sprang to her eyes when he said this. She never expected to be treated this way. Her father-in-law had always been courteous and kind to her. She was shaking all over. Did one unobserved custom really invalidate all the years she'd spent with Kumani, all of the life they'd built together? Yes, the ceremonial practices for the customary marriage had not been completed, and they were not yet legally married either but they had two children, Tumi and Lindiwe, aged eleven and nine, and they had been living together in the Aspen Hills Nature Estate for years. They were a family.

Her father-in-law was still talking, but all she heard was a ringing in her ears. At last she heard him say, 'We'll come by tomorrow. Make sure you are at home.'

When he hung up, she went to the master bedroom that she had shared with Kumani, curled into a ball, pulled the comforter over her and blocked out the world. She cried because she missed him so much, and because she felt utterly alone.

The next evening, a Sunday, her father-in-law showed up with her brother-in-law, Fakazi, to collect some of her husband's clothes for the burial rituals. They gave themselves a free pass to go upstairs to the master bedroom and rummage through the closets.

She kept quiet because the children were already asleep in the next rooms and she didn't want to wake them with raised voices.

It was then that they pulled the three-piece navy suit from a hanger. The one Kumani would have worn on their wedding day if he hadn't been taken from her so prematurely. 'This will do,' her father-in-law said with his bony curled fingers rubbing the material.

She thought he wanted it to bury her husband in it. If she only knew then that old man Ntimani planned to take the suit for him-self, she would not have left them alone to continue their task while she went downstairs to wipe her eyes and blow her nose.

When the men eventually came down, she saw that Fakazi's

arms were loaded with her late husband's clothes – more than they could ever need for any rituals. They had also helped themselves to other possessions of Kumani's, such as a laptop, slung over her father-in-law's shoulder, and a stereo, which he clutched with both arms.

'Where are you taking these things?' she demanded, casting off any semblance of respect for the supposed men of the family.

Old man Ntimani sniffed indignantly. His lips were right underneath his nose, very close to it – so close, in fact, he could easily sniff along his upper lip. 'These things belonged to my son. You have no claim on them, just as you had no claim on him.'

'This is outrageous! I have to ask you to put down those possessions and leave this house immediately.'

'We will not put them down. But we will leave . . . For now . . .' the old man said as they exited. Fakazi looked her briefly in the eyes as they left, then looked away. He had a childlike face, covered in sweat, with big eyes that gazed at her with a challenge in them. She was most surprised at him. Marang shuddered when she thought of how close she had been to Fakazi when his brother was still alive. Then, her brother-in-law had been a placid, slightly withdrawn character. She recalled, with dull sadness but without bitterness, how attentive Fakazi had been towards her. It was almost unbelievable to Marang how brutal some people could be, and how the most refined manners often concealed savage coarseness.

Marang did not attend the burial of her husband, not willing to make a scene or face the hostile in-laws, not willing to subject her children to that.

She was disappointed in herself that she had accepted their marginalisation of her from the burial and hadn't acted more decisively when they pilfered her husband's possessions. She was still confined to the silences that culture and patriarchy prescribed. Deep down, she was devastated by the weight of her in-laws' rejection. Not even Kumani's sisters, Rea and Dineo, had reached out to her.

A month later, one Saturday morning, old man Ntimani and Fakazi showed up again. She sent the children to go play in the back garden and ordered them not to disturb the grown-ups' discussion in the living room.

As she took her seat, she fixed her gaze on old man Ntimani, who was sitting straight-backed, a few metres in front of her. Fakazi was sitting silently to the side. Ntimani's face and body looked small and shrunken in on itself. It was all bones, veins, skin and muscle, with not a single scrap of fat. His skull was stripped of hair by mange and old age.

Her father-in-law grinned maliciously at her, revealing a mouthful of rotting teeth. 'We came here to tell you that you have to leave and go back to your people by next week,' he said. 'You can't live here any more.'

'With all due respect, Papa Ntimane, this is my house.'

'My son built this house, and you are not a Ntimani.'

'I built it together with my husband. And what about my children? Are they no longer part of this Ntimani family either? They are Kumani's daughters and this is their family.'

'You should have thought about that when you killed my son.'

A look of disgust swept across his face. His breathing had grown a little ragged, and he kept wiping sweat off his forehead and scalp with his handkerchief.

'What?' Marang was rattled by this accusation. 'But he died in a car accident, and you both know it.' She looked to Fakazi for help, but he remained silent.

'You bewitched him. How does one die alone in a car carrying four people? The rest came out with minor scratches and they didn't even spend a day in hospital.'

Marang tried to keep calm, not believing her ears. She inclined her face towards old man Ntimani to keep him from looking around, and said, with a voice admittedly trembling and uncontrolled, 'And why should I be the one to blame in that circumstance? Maybe the colleagues he was driving with in the front passenger seat and the back had their seatbelts on – who knows?'

'From next week Friday, Fakazi will live here. We can't allow you to continue enjoying the fruits of my son's labour after you have killed him.'

She watched the two visitors through tear-filled eyes. Those cruel words made her feel crushed, worthless.

'But my husband died while we were still planning our white wedding. You know very well that he died in a car accident along the N1 to Pretoria.'

'Yes, you bewitched him before the performance of rituals and the planned wedding. But rituals are a direct communication with our ancestors. Ask your parents and they may teach you that marriage in our culture entails certain rituals. It was not done in your case because you killed my son before those rituals.'

'This is my home, I'm not leaving. I have nowhere to go.'

'You are definitely going.'

'Where do you expect me to go?'

'We don't care where you go. You can go back to your parents' home, or you can find a new husband and live with him. You can go anywhere you want. But you can't live here. You're a stranger to us.'

Marang buried her face in her hands. She wished she could fall down and break into pieces.

'Why do you hate me so much?'

'You are not married to my son. You don't have the blessings from this family, nor do we recognise you. You have to leave the house. And, as I say, my son here, Fakazi, will take over this house and the one in Hartbees. If you refuse to go, we will force you out. You *will* go.'

After the father and son had left, Marang tried carrying on as normal, for the sake of the children. But as soon as the girls had gone to bed, she let the tears stream down her face until her eyes were red and her face puffy with weeping and despair. What would Kumani have said if he could see her then. He had always maintained that she had a beautiful face with her wide black eyes. She missed him so much.

She called her mother, Kele, to come over the following evening. They went upstairs to the balcony of the double-storey house and opened a bottle of wine. From this vantage point they could see the sprawling estate as Marang filled their glasses before relating to her mother all that had happened.

'You can't give up now,' her mother said. 'As a woman, you must confront all sorts of perils as bravely as possible.'

'But what can I do, Mama? I have tried to remain calm.'

'Your calmness is the main problem. You cannot be silent forever. Silence is good for a few moments. But when it stretches out for too long, it gives others an advantage over you. This is a strange kind of a war where you cannot afford to have fragile fists and a heart of sponge.'

'I'm scared,' she groaned and blinked away her tears.

'You need to live with this chaos inside you for a while, Marang. After this experience, your body will give birth to a dancing star. It is clear that if you do nothing about it, you will be succumbing to your in-laws' endless control over your body and reality.'

'These people will kill me.'

'Of course that father- and brother-in-law will try to intimidate you with their maleness because being a male is a privileged identity,' Kele said, sipping her glass of red wine. 'They are hellbent on destroying you. They will continue to use their position to intimidate and punish you for nothing. But the law will protect you.'

'How, Mama? We were not legally married.'

'You have to challenge this unfairness and greyness, this ambiguity of the customary marriage. I want to introduce you to Advocate Luka. He is very good. He helped my colleague at the Department of Labour last year with a similar case of trouble with the in-laws.'

'Will dragging them to court not make them hate me more? Is there not some other way to do it?'

'It does not sound like you can reason with them any other way.

They seem to hate you, even though you did nothing wrong. Nothing at all. Of course, they are lazy people who were waiting for your husband to die so that they could claim his property ahead of you. In fact, I would not have been surprised if they killed their son because they wanted to inherit his property. As a matter of survival, you have to decide to treat everybody in your husband's family as the enemy.'

Marang nodded silently, and mother and daughter sat for a while, lifting their eyes towards the sky where pink clouds were forming around the setting sun. Marang topped up their glasses.

'It's amazing how marriage works,' she said. 'One minute you are treated as desirable by the in-laws, and the next you are perceived as intimidating.'

'You have to move on, Marang,' Kele said when they had drunk two bottles of wine and Marang had called an Uber to take her mother home. 'Don't tie yourself to your husband's corpse for too long. After your father died, I also thought it was the end of the world.'

Looking at him now as they wait outside the courtroom, Marang is thankful that Fakazi hadn't shown up that night after her mother had left because she was indeed a little drunk and not in full control of all her faculties. She shudders to think what might have happened. But he did arrive at her door quite late the next night.

At first, she thought he was being sincere when he sat down next to her on her living-room couch and told her that he was so sorry about everything that was going on between their families. The expression in his eyes was one of sadness when he took her hand.

'The last thing I want is for you and the girls to be put out of your home,' he said.

'Oh, Fakazi, I'm so glad to hear you say that,' she said. 'I'm so glad you are on my side. You have always been a friend to me.'

He squeezed her hand tighter and said, 'I have a solution to all our troubles, my dear. You and Tumi and Lindiwe can stay on in the house with me when I take possession of it.'

She saw the change in his eyes, the undisguised lust there, and tried to pull her hand away.

'Come upstairs with me and we will seal the deal,' he purred like a cat ready to pounce on a mouse.

'Fakazi, no!' She stomped on his foot with the high heel of her shoe as hard as she could. He yelled out and let go of her hand to grab his sneaker. She jumped up. 'Your brother has been dead for little more than a month. How dare you!'

Fakazi's eyes were bulging and he got up slowly, putting his weight on the foot she hadn't attacked. 'Oh, you know I've always wanted you, Marang. Don't play dumb. And you've always been leading me on with those smiles and hugs, rubbing yourself up against me.'

'You're sick in the head! My affection for you is that of a sister for a brother.'

'Oh please, you were never even fully married to my brother. You are no sister of mine. And besides, even if you were, according to tradition I'm allowed to take my deceased brother's wife.'

The way he stared at her felt like a physical assault. 'Get out of my house!' she yelled.

He took a menacing step in her direction.

'I'm warning you, I'll call the police,' she said.

He sneered at her and took another step forwards.

'What's going on, Mommy?' Tumi had appeared at the top of the stairs, rubbing sleep from her eyes.

Fakazi seemed to get a hold of himself at the sight of the little girl. 'Nothing, sweetie, I was just leaving,' he said. But as he pushed past Marang, he whispered, 'This is not over; consider it just the first round.'

'I'm not afraid of you,' she said with the fierceness of a lioness not only protecting herself but also her cubs. She was eyeballing him inches from her face and she looked right through him. 'I may look like a coward to you. But from time to time I suffer from outbreaks of bravery.'

Fakazi looked at Marang and he bit his lips in annoyance. 'Your "bravery" will put you and your children on the street. Consider my offer.'

She did not know where her burst of courage had come from, but it soon fled when she locked the front door behind him with trembling hands. Then she made sure all the windows were closed and the alarm activated.

Tumi went back to sleep as soon as she was tucked into bed, but in her own room Marang felt like the linen was fighting with her as she tossed and turned. When she finally fell asleep, she dreamt of Fakazi coming at her through the bedroom window, brandishing a hunting knife.

In the morning, she contacted the advocate her mother had suggested.

Fakazi came round a few more times, but she never opened the door for him, and she didn't answer his texts. Two months after her husband was buried, Fakazi and his two sisters brought a dodgy locksmith to Marang's Aspen Hills Nature Estate mansion one afternoon. The locksmith helped them to get into the house and Marang was chilled to the bone to later learn that Dineo knew the alarm code – Kumani's birth date. What if she had shared it with Fakazi and her nightmare about him had really come true? The intent of her in-laws that day was malicious enough. They used the locksmith to change the locks to her house.

Marang's children were still at school and she was at work. Around three in the afternoon, when the children came back from school, they found the gate to the house locked. The girls' keys no longer worked. It started to rain heavily. As they stood under the tree outside the yard, their books and school uniforms were soaked. She arrived at five and immediately took them to the safety of her mother's house.

From that day onwards, Marang had been openly at war with her in-laws. With the help of Advocate Luka, she went to court. She wanted to refute their claims against her inheritance. She wanted protection against the malevolent spirit of her in-laws.

Now they have been let into the courtroom and the judge is speaking. He is reading his verdict. Marang shuts her eyes tight, and hopes and prays.

'The marriage is valid,' the judge says.

Marang lets out a little involuntary squeal. She makes a muted clapping sound with her hands. For the first time in many months, she smiles broadly.

'Customary marriage is dynamic, flexible and not stagnant,' the judge continues. 'The moment you welcomed her family after paying the lobolo, you validated the marriage between Marang Kole and Kumani Ntimane. The counter-application to have the marriage invalidated by this court is therefore dismissed.'

As the judge speaks the last sentence, Marang looks groggily around as if to orientate herself. She sees her in-laws glow with shared rage. But her cries of joy and excitement last for many minutes.

Marang and her mother walk out of the court like she is a patient cured of a tumour.

'God is great. It is over now,' Kele says as they reach the steps outside the court entrance.

'I pray to the god of peace, serenity, creation and wisdom that this thing is truly finally over and that they don't come with any more tricks.'

'It's over. The only trick they can try is witchcraft. That will not work, because you're God's daughter.'

'I just want to live peacefully with my girls,' Marang says as they get into her car. 'After this court ruling, I will try to sell the house and move away somewhere we can start anew.'

Driving southwards to her mother's house to collect her girls and take them home to Aspen (the in-laws had been ordered to vacate the house and give the keys to her lawyer), she puts her cupped palm out of the window of her car. The fresh breeze ruffles her Brazilian hair. She lowers the window some more. Driving with one hand, she lets her right arm hang over the hot side of the car.

The words of the judge keep echoing in her mind.

'The marriage is valid,' she sighs with relief.

FOR YOU, I'D STEAL A GOAT

The Berlin lockdown is announced in March 2020. Zwai and I find ourselves trapped in the city. The flights back to South Africa are cancelled immediately and indefinitely.

We arrived just over three months ago. Most of the performances of our play, *Nailed,* at the English Theatre Berlin, Kreuzberg, were sold out. Our host was also in the middle of securing us a deal to perform in Hamburg and a few other German cities.

Come March, everything changes. Our shows are cancelled. The German chancellor announces lockdown regulations. All theatre activities are suspended. We are supposed to wear masks and practise social distancing at all times. The usual buzzing Berlin streets are empty. Pubs and bars are closed. Everyone is buying provisions in bulk that will sustain them for months. There are long queues for toilet paper and tinned foods in the supermarkets. Shelves are emptied. No one knows what will happen.

We all sink into a great depression. My friend Zwai and I are panicking. I experience insomnia. I often look at the moon. It feels like it has a hole in the middle. I'm sure that I'm going mad.

Sometimes I wake up convinced that I'm already home in Piet Retief and living through the dawn of a long age of progress and peace. When this happens, as it often does, I start talking in isiZulu with my girlfriend, Ursula, until she stops me.

We are in the middle of April. Still, Zwai and I are waiting. There are no flights back home. The two of us are only barely equipped with the German language. In this present predicament, we rely on our host for a place to stay and an allowance to buy food. In the meantime, perfectly useless thoughts crowd my head.

Almost every day Zwai and I hear only sad news from home. People we know are struggling in lockdown with no means to earn money. Extended families who were dependent on one person to support them now have nothing. There are people we know who are sick and some have died. I fear the worst is yet to come in my home country. At night I'm restless, either half asleep or half awake. I can be woken up by hunger at regular intervals, or be kept half awake by anxieties and unclear hopes.

It is a Friday afternoon in April. The three of us, Zwai, Ursula and me, are sitting on our Am Tempelhofer ground-floor balcony. I've just had a conversation with my father at home via WhatsApp call. I'm in high spirits, maybe because of the combination of the call and the joint we are smoking. We bought it at Görlitzer Park that morning. We are also drinking my favourite Jever beer to kill the slow-moving time while waiting for the German chancellor to announce more Covid-19 protocols. My small JBL boom speaker is playing 'Yellow' by Coldplay. We lie on the reclining chairs, passing the joint from one mouth to another.

Ursula's head is thrown back. Her mouth is half open, eyes fixed upwards, the position that indicates that she means to sing. We have been together for nine months. We met during a past visit to Berlin when I also came to do a theatre performance. Around July last year, to be precise. She is a photographer who was sent to do publicity shots of my show. She did it for quick money, but she prefers more artistic photographic pursuits and has exhibited her work in some small galleries.

I'm looking up at the grey afternoon sky. I'm thankful for the pure air, thankful for the sun – although faint – thankful to be alive in a foreign city. But my predicament is weighing heavily on my mind. My livelihood has been taken away from me. I have no way to earn an income, and this thought is bringing Ursula's mother's voice to my mind: 'Can you make a living out of it?' she asked when she heard what my occupation was.

Now our entire visit to her parents in Biesdorf a few weeks ago is running through my mind. Unlike my family and friends in South Africa, who are not allowed to visit each other in this time of lockdown, Germany has not restricted movement between households. It was my first time meeting Ursula's parents. The introduction was not as pleasant as we would have loved. Well, I was okay with it. Ursula didn't like it at all.

Ursula and her mother were sitting outside the family home with their knees almost touching. Petra sat on a chair made of pallets and Ursula and I next to each other on a wooden bench. Only the fine wrinkles on her forehead and at the corners of her mouth showed that Petra was approaching sixty. 'So, you two want to go and live in Africa or here in Germany?' she asked.

Joachim, Ursula's stepdad, was resting on his elbow and listening from the other pallet chair. He had small bluish eyes, lost beneath his bushy eyebrows. His puffy cheeks and longish nose were the colour of an overripe tomato.

'We have not reached that decision yet, Mom,' Ursula said.

Petra turned her head to look at me. 'What do you do besides performing, Lungelo?'

'But I already told you, Mom,' protested Ursula. She reached across her seat, slung her arm around me and pulled me closer. I, in turn, slid my hand lightly down her back, sweeping it over her buttocks so slyly that her mother and stepdad didn't notice.

'It's okay, babe,' I said to Ursula. 'Let me answer that. Well, I'm a performer and nothing else.'

'That's your only job?' I felt Petra's glare on me like the heat of a blistering sun.

Joachim listened, nodded and took a sip of his drink. The way he sat on his chair with his legs spread apart signalled that he had no intention of getting up, or saying a word, or moving. He would only sit there belching his beer.

'So far, yes. It's my only job.'

'Can you make a living out of it?'

'Well, sometimes. Except now because of the virus. Our shows are cancelled.'

'So, both of you are freelance artists? And you think this is enough to sustain you?'

Ursula's face flushed red. Her lips pulled back in a snarl. She started to blink in a terrifying way. I wrapped my arm around her waist. She looked at her mother for a moment. Then she looked at me for any sign of annoyance.

'Of course we will survive. Don't worry about us.' Her eyes hinted at an unspoken secret between us. It was the silent floating spirit of lovers.

'Of course in a fantasy anything is possible,' Petra said. 'I think you guys are suffering from a belated teenage hormone problem if you cannot see that you need proper jobs to survive.'

At this declaration, Ursula burst out, 'Mom, please stop it.'

'Stop what? Speaking the truth? I ask you in all seriousness. I want to know if this is the kind of life you would like to have in the future. As a mother, I'm only trying to understand how the two of you are going to live without a proper job. That's all.'

'We can't all be working at the bank, you know.'

Ursula's stepdad clenched his fist with a pugnacious expression. It was as if he were ready to push Petra into the house and tell her to shut up.

'Why are you so set on spoiling our visit?' Ursula demanded.

This time Petra weighed her words carefully and cleared her throat. 'Ursula, you're my only daughter. Is it wrong for a mother to ask her daughter for—'

'It is impolite. In fact, quite shameful.'

'What do you want in life, Ursula?' Petra said in a commanding voice, as if she had been practising the question in front of the mirror before we came. 'That is a fair question, isn't it?'

'No.'

'But you—' Petra's lips stopped in mid-sentence. She saw my head turn, eyes narrowed with interest. Her brow glistened with a sheen of sweat. She tried to wipe it with the pad of her thumb. It seemed that she was trying to blur the embarrassment of the whole thing. The more seconds passed, the better able she was to do so.

'I didn't mean to—'

'Mom, just shut up, will you? I have taken you for quite a sensible individual, but today you seem set on your embarrassing mood.'

Petra was quiet. At the same time, the blood of the setting sun spilled out on the western horizon. The trees were slowly turning dark and casting deep shadows. Minute by minute, the shadows lengthened.

Ursula rose to her feet and dropped her hands. She looked at the trees overhanging the house and heaved a sigh of impatience.

'Let's go, babe,' she said, tapping me lightly on the shoulder.

'Now?'

'Yes. Now.'

As I was about to follow her out of the gate, Petra called me back and gave me a bottle of wine. The gesture was so unexpected.

'Please have this. Don't worry about us much. We always fight because she is always overreacting. Do you think I was impolite?'

She then looked solemnly into my face as she was talking to me, repeating the word 'impolite' three times: 'Me, impolite? I was never impolite. Why would I be impolite?'

I didn't say a word. A little hesitantly, I gave my full agreement with a nod. Petra furrowed her brow, as though looking for words that she wanted to say.

Ursula and I took the U5 train back to the city. We were halfway towards the Biesdorf-Süd station when I smelled the rain.

'I'm sorry that my mother interrogated you like that. She acted more like an immigration officer than a mother,' said Ursula, sounding frustrated, almost angry. 'And I'm also sorry that my stepdad kept looking at you a little longer than necessary. He is like that.'

'To be honest, I didn't mind that. It didn't bother me at all. But anyway, thank you for protecting me from some of her intrusive questions.'

Ursula tried to explain to me her relationship with her mother as far as her tongue would allow her. 'The problem is that my mother seems very dissatisfied with me. She is always finding things to criticise in me. I am forever being unfair to her. Sometimes it seems I annoy her with every breath and step because I don't have a successful career according to her.'

She ended up going on an emotional rampage that lasted until we reached Kreuzberg. I responded with yeses and nos just to fill in my silence.

On our balcony, Ursula passes me the joint, bringing me back to the present. I suck on the zol, inhaling and slowly blowing out smoke. What I imagine to be a good plan crosses my mind. I want to share it with both Zwai and Ursula.

'I think this thing needs some ancestral intervention,' I say.

'What do you mean?' asks Ursula.

'This thing is simple. We must get a goat to slaughter here in Berlin and appease our ancestors.'

At first, Ursula laughs at the way I express my idea. I pass the joint to Zwai. The light winks out of Ursula's eyes. A short, uncomfortable silence follows. Ursula shoots me one of her smouldering looks. The words vaporise on my tongue.

'Are you okay, bro?' Zwai asks. 'Are you aware we are in Berlin and not in Piet Retief?'

'Maybe he is daydreaming again,' says Ursula. 'Wake up, Lungelo.'

'I'm serious about this. I have been thinking about it since the lockdown started.'

Now both Ursula and Zwai appear shocked. Ursula turns her

face up. She squints and breathes like the city is running out of air. 'What? Are you out of your mind, Lungelo? You can't be serious. You're joking, right?'

'I'm not joking. I'm dead serious. As I say, I have been thinking a lot about this since the start of the lockdown and our cancelled shows. I have seen some goats at that small zoo along the Bergmannstrasse right by Victoria Park. I think I can steal one nice goat that we can slaughter sometime this week.'

'Oh my God. You're out of your mind. Stop smoking so much weed,' says Zwai, the smoke from the zol passing beneath his nostrils. 'This is Germany, my friend, not South Africa, in case you have forgotten. You can't steal. There are surveillance systems everywhere. Do you want to go to jail and jeopardise our chances of ever performing in German theatres again just for stealing a goat?'

'Our choices are limited while here in Berlin, my friend. I spend sleepless nights worrying whether I will be able to make it back home alive. A goat will be able to communicate a message to the ancestors.'

'You are being pessimistic,' says Ursula. 'Everything will be over in a few weeks. This lockdown is not forever.'

'In two weeks, you think? I don't think so. And that's exactly why we need to communicate with our ancestors to open the borders so that we can get the hell out of here safely.'

'But still I don't understand. What good does slaughtering a poor goat do? And why a goat, specifically?'

'Ursula, my love, I want to introduce you properly to my ancestors. I can only do it with a goat.'

'So, your ancestors can only eat a goat – not a rabbit, not a duck, not a turkey or a chicken, but a goat?'

'Yes. We must find a goat. Otherwise our Africa will be nothing more than a distant rumour, my darling. We will never see our beautiful landscapes again. Do you remember that I promised to take you there?' We have been planning to visit South Africa. I promised to introduce her to my parents in Piet Retief. That is the promise I will keep. Maybe after that we can take our relationship to another level. 'Last week my cousin succumbed to Covid. Today Zwai got the bad news that his grandmother is in the hospital. We need a goat to communicate with our ancestors so that they can show us the way.'

'I know,' Zwai says, 'but at the moment I don't miss Africa. I miss performing in the theatre here, and not those landscapes of baobabs, acacias, and tall grasses.'

'Exactly why we need a goat, my friend.'

'Well, if the goat can help to get us back into the theatre again, then I'm in.'

'We need to make those euros.'

Ursula looked sceptical. 'No ancestor will hear you from this foreign place with a stupid goat.'

'Shh, you cannot talk like that, Ursula, my love. You will pay for it in the next world if you continue using expressions like that. Ancestors are gods – omnipresent, omniscient and omnipotent.'

'So, they support the killing of an innocent beautiful animal? No way I'm going along with that idea.'

'Well, it is my tradition to sacrifice a goat for my ancestors when I face challenges like this.'

'Why is it always according to your tradition?'

'I think my ancestors will be angry if I don't announce our love for each other to them properly through the blood of the goat.'

Zwai rolls another joint and we all lapse into silent contemplation.

One cold afternoon, a week after my goat proposal, Ursula surprises Zwai and me. We are in the sitting room, surrounded by a cloud of weed smoke.

She comes closer to me, but uncertainly. I can feel the uneasiness in her heart in spite of the weed and the great quantities of wine Zwai and I have consumed.

'Babe, I've been thinking hard about it. I know where to get you a goat.'

'Are you sure about it, babe?' I ask, taking a step backwards with a smile of disbelief.

There is the sound of her anxious breathing. Zwai is rolling a joint on the couch.

'Well, I'm sure.'

Her words take a slow second to arrive at my ear and sink in.

'How are you going to get it?' Zwai asks.

'I have an uncle who lives near Wuhletal. He has a few goats on his small farm. He uses their milk to produce cheese.'

'Good shot. My ancestors will be pleased with a cheese-producing German goat. It will be the first they ever taste since they were buried,' I say.

'Yeah. We can steal a goat for you from my uncle's small farm. The problem may be to get the goat here.'

'Wow, thank you, love. That's one of the reasons I love you. You don't discriminate against my ancestors.'

Zwai burns the joint. Ursula darts over to the window and flings it open with febrile hands. She doesn't seem to care how cold it might be outside. She stands by the window taking deep breaths.

Zwai passes the joint to her.

'Love makes people ridiculous,' she says as she takes a puff. 'Just look at me now. I'm unashamedly already agreeing to the slaughter of my uncle's stolen goat for your ancestors. It is against my own ancestors' protestant principles. What if I get caught?'

'Don't worry, my love. We have Zwai, the biggest thief from Soweto, here. He'll never get caught. Besides, when you come to Africa we will steal a whole sheep for your Protestant ancestors. That's if they don't eat goat.'

'My Protestant ancestors only need a prayer and not goat meat.'

'Wow, are they vegans?'

'Maybe. But for you, I'd steal a goat,' she says as she passes the joint to me.

'Praise the Lord. For God promised men like me that good and obedient and loving wives would be found in all corners of the world, especially Berlin. It's not by coincidence that we met, my love. It was through the mercy of God and my ancestors.'

'Praise the Lord.'

'What about people like me who have not found love yet?' asks Zwai.

'Of course God made the world round for people like you. That's why you cannot find a loving woman in the four corners in which God put them.'

'What did I say to you the other day? I told you that anything is possible after a man and a woman have laughed together and shared their nakedness. Look at what Ursula is willing to sacrifice for you now.'

'Just the mention of that beautiful name is enough to make me feel more of a man, my friend.'

On Wednesday evening, Ursula, Zwai and I decide to take a drive to Wuhletal. Ursula has borrowed her mother's car to make the goat transportation easy and unsuspicious. We are smoking weed inside the vehicle. The way we blow our smoke upwards from our noses and mouths indicates in particular a great nervousness on our part. 'Wicked game' by Chris Isaak is playing and enhancing our fearful mood. Ursula is singing along.

'You two must know that I'm not catching the damn goat for you. You will have to do that part by yourselves,' Ursula says after a while.

'What if we get caught?' Zwai asks.

'Then I will help my uncle's wife to shoot you,' she says jokingly.

'Can't we just ask for the damn goat?'

'Are you crazy?' I ask. 'Who in their generous good mind would donate a cheese-producing goat to two Africans who will in turn donate it to their dead ancestors?'

The sun has almost sunk behind the hills when we arrive. Dusk has painted the sky pink and purple. Crops and yellow weeds blanket the hillside. The wildflowers and grass reach upwards. The trees are still sparsely clothed with young leaves, the whole earth is covered with fresh greenery, and all the fields are fragrant with spring. A little star shines in the distance, stark against the forest rushing past with its dark trees. The Fleetwood Mac song 'Everywhere' starts to play. Ursula reduces the volume.

'Here is the plan. My uncle is away, so I will pretend to be talking to his wife. I've already lied to my uncle's wife that I will pass by her place for a few minutes on my way from Kaulsdorf. One or both of you will sneak behind the house and carry the goat into the car from the pen that they are kept in. Be quick.'

'What about the dogs?' I ask. 'Does he have dogs?'

'Of course he does. As far as I know, he keeps them inside the house after sunset.'

The car comes to a stop near a farmhouse. It is beginning to rain. Before she gets out of the car, Ursula points at the kraal behind the farmhouse. Zwai licks his lips and clears his throat. Ursula's face twitches. Her eyes flick from Zwai to me.

'I'm sure you have stolen many goats before in Piet Retief, but be careful,' she warns me. 'This is a German goat.'

'Say we catch it,' Zwai asks. 'Who is going to slaughter it?'

'Don't look at me. I have not slaughtered a goat before. It's up to you two. Besides, it was your idea to get a goat. Did you expect me to get a butcher as well?'

Zwai and I wait for Ursula to go inside the house before we get out of the car. The rain is falling hard. My wet clothes cling to me, and I feel the sudden weight of them. In the dark, I tackle the goat by its head. It bleats once, but luckily it is drowned out by the heavy rain and the sound of thunder. I clamp its mouth shut. Zwai gets it by its hind legs. It's also not as big as we thought. It's a he-goat.

The whole operation takes less than fifteen minutes. I see Ursula standing with her uncle's wife on the farmhouse veranda, their heads facing each other, in intimate conversation. The goat is already in the boot and we are in the car. It is still raining hard. Zwai is rolling a joint.

'Just so that we are clear. I'm not going to slaughter the damn goat,' says Zwai as he licks the edge of the rolling paper.

'Then you are not going to eat the meat,' I say with no trace of humour, no irony. 'It's as simple as that, my dear friend.'

'Of course I'm going to eat the meat.'

'Then you will have to slaughter the goat with me.'

When Ursula gets back into the car, she plays David Bowie's 'Heroes'. She looks hyper as she sings along. The song is certainly telling her things that are making her heart drunk with joy.

'*Oh we can be heroes, just for one day*,' she sings along.

It is around eleven at night when we arrive in Kreuzberg with the goat. We carry it upstairs wrapped in my jacket so that it will look like an injured dog from far away. Luckily there is no one at the lift as we take the stairs. Inside our flat, Zwai and I put the goat in the bathroom, ready for slaughter. First, Zwai fetches two Jever beers from the fridge and opens them. Without hesitating, without making a face, like a studied drinker, with his round bulging eyes and bobbing Adam's apple, he empties his beer in one go.

'Now we can slaughter the damn goat.'

It looks like some sedative is wearing off and he now feels himself surging with energy. Next to me, Ursula shows no sign of fear at seeing Zwai and me carrying knives. She leans her elbows on the balcony rail, her hand supporting her head, and looks out. She seems to be swaying to an inaudible beat. She pretends to be paying no attention to the imminent slaughter.

As I enter the bathroom where the goat is, my cheeks burn. Guilt courses through me. All of a sudden, the goat scans me and the door with its condemned beady eyes. As if propelled by an excess of mistrust, it bolts through the door to the balcony where Ursula is standing smoking. Clambering between the few flower pots and the chair, it leaps onto the railing and into the street. Ursula gives a little scream. She is bewildered and even beginning to show unmistakable signs of fear. I look at her and Zwai, trying to summon up the handful of courage I possess. Sweat is pouring off me.

Ursula looks uncertainly over the balcony. She covers her eyes with both hands before she lets out a brief, shrill laugh. She moves close to me, turns round as if to see what impact the escape of the goat has had on our faces.

'What happened?' She is breathing hard through her open mouth.

Not bothering to say a word, Zwai points with his index finger at the goat that is by now moving along the road. He shakes his head. He is stuck in an upright position, watching in astonishment.

'The German goat is resisting the knife.'

Ursula's mouth is open. She is now standing next to him as though nailed to the ground, and in complete disorientation. Zwai's lips are pressed together, his eyes wide open. Ursula looks at me and then smiles in a way that a grown-up person might smile at a foolish child. She is caressing a flower that the goat left uprooted from a flower pot. She closes it in her cupped hands and then opens the petals with faltering fingers.

'I guess I have just obligingly opened a door to the charming incarnation of evil,' Ursula says to no one in particular.

ACKNOWLEDGEMENTS

'Johustlerburg Prison Cell' first appeared in the anthology *Joburg Noir*, edited by Niq Mhlongo (Jacana, 2020).

'Fireplace' first appeared in the anthology *Hauntings*, edited by Niq Mhlongo (Jacana, 2021).

ABOUT THE AUTHOR

Niq Mhlongo is an award-winning author from Soweto. He holds a BA degree from Wits University, majoring in African Literature and Political Studies. *For You, I'd Steal a Goat* is his third short story collection, following *Affluenza* and *Soweto, Under the Apricot Tree*. The latter was awarded the 2019 Herman Charles Bosman Prize and the 2019 Nadine Gordimer Short Story Award, one of the South African Literary Awards (SALAs). He has also published four novels, namely *Dog Eat Dog*, *After Tears*, *Way Back Home* and *Paradise in Gaza*. The Spanish translation of *Dog Eat Dog* won the Mar de Letras prize in 2006. In addition, Mhlongo has edited a collection of essays titled *Black Tax: Burden or Ubuntu* and two short story anthologies, *Joburg Noir* and *Hauntings*.